A BlackWyrm Book
Louisville, Kentucky

THE RAINBOW CONNECTION

A BlackWyrm Book
BlackWyrm Publishing
10307 Chimney Ridge Ct, Louisville, KY 40299

Printed in the United States of America.

ISBN: 978-0-9820067-1-9
LCCN: 2008942314
Cover by Jesse Parrotti
Edited by Dave Mattingly and Jason Walters

First edition: February 2009
Second edition: August 2012

The police station was a chaotic jumble of scales and species. A horse, full sized, with a captain's insignia on a sash around his neck, was dispensing orders to three munchkins in uniforms vaguely resembling those of English Bobbies from the turn of the prior century. A bored looking woman in a uniform seemingly composed of gold lame and glitter idly waved a wand over piles of paperwork, which dutifully sorted itself as she stifled a yawn and glanced at the clock. A complex automaton of some sort was standing partially disassembled against a wall, while a mechanic poked at it was what could only be described as a steam-powered wrench. Near the door, a dented bucket sat precariously balanced atop a pile of brooms.

Matt and Bobbi looked around, confused, when the pile of brooms animated itself and walked towards them. The bucket head turned, revealing eyes that were expressive and clearly painted on. It spoke, the voice issuing from the 'head,' but no mouth was visible.

"Sergeant Whisk, on duty today. Can I help you with something?"

My sanity, thought Matt, but tried to soldier on.

"Uh… I guess so… um…" He fumbled with the photographs for a second, then found the clearest one he could. "Do you, ah, know this person?"

Surprisingly agile hands of straw gently took the picture from Matt, the hundreds of small strands moving with grace and certainty. The painted, yet living, eyes, narrowed, and then, somehow, the strange and alien face managed to take on a look of very real sadness.

"Loko."

Bobbi blinked. "He was crazy? Or *we're* crazy?" Certainly, she'd been thinking it, but to have it confirmed by what had to be a delusion….

The bucket-head blinked in confusion of its own. "Hm? No, this is Loko. Lokorian Balgorad, to be formal, but we all knew him as just Loko. He had a small shop a block or two from here. Sold shoes. He was arrested for unlicensed wizardry, oh, about six months ago… About two months ago, his wife tried to visit him, and was told he'd 'escaped.'" Sergeant Whisk snorted, an amazing feat give the lack of any nose, or, it seemed any internal structure to the bucket. "No one just 'escapes' from that place."

Dedicated to:

My wife,
who puts up with me.
This is no small thing.

My cats,
who "help" me
in more ways than can be documented.
(Anyone want a cat or two?)

The Vault Writer's Group,
which seemed to like this enough
to encourage me to finish it.

It all started with the dead munchkin. Well, maybe a little bit before that...

The dealer's room was a celebration of capitalism on acid. Everywhere money changed hands frantically, weeks or months of wages tossed away on all manner of useless gewgaws, from mediocre books signed by mediocre authors to overpriced replicas of non-existent weapons. The crowd was filled with all kinds and manners of beings, from armor-clad science-fiction mercenaries to women who were both nearly attractive and nearly dressed.

Matt Anders surveyed the crowd, noting a wide range of would-be aliens, cyborgs, and monsters. All of them were fairly palpably fake. That was good. Too authentic, and the INS guys might show, demanding that *you* take your head off, or else *they* would. Immigration laws were getting stricter every day. Congress was about to require DNA tests for all employment – not that that would weed out any of the truly human refugees.

At least that's not my job, he thought glumly. *I don't have to go telling people, "Sorry, we know where you came from is hell. Tough luck, you can't stay here." All* I *do*, he thought, *is round up greedy nerds*.

He looked around at the rows and rows of dealers. *And on that note, this is a target-rich environment.*

He glanced down at the business card in his hand: "Big Frank's Comics And More!" On the back was scribbled the somewhat cryptic notation: "G-820." Matt glanced up. Aisle G was one row over. He pushed through the thick crowd until he found the booth he was looking for.

It was mobbed by an assortment of aficionados of obscure videos trawling over the densely packed rows of tapes and discs like ants over a corpse. Every so often, one would give a little grunt of excitement and lunge frantically for one item or another, adding it to the pile in his arms. The rotund, bearded gentleman behind the boxes spent most of his time arguing minor points of trivia with all the passion of a debate over nuclear disarmament, and seemed annoyed when his pontifications on the topic of computer graphics or filming on-location but off-world were interrupted by someone eager to pay him hundreds of dollars for a few slim pieces of plastic.

Matt checked out the display. Most of it was legal or quasi-legal – unaired pilots, foreign programs not yet released in the states, that sort of thing. Theoretically, he could pin him for those alone, but that wasn't his job. Nothing here seemed to be under his particular purview, but the tipoff was supposed to be reliable…

He sighed. He'd have to break into the conversation and talk to the man.

"…so anyway, I know it's supposed to be the *real* Arrakis, or close enough, but, man, the worms just looked so *wrong*. There's such a thing as too much authenticity, you know? And they had to splice in all the actors… huh? Can I help you, man?"

"Yes." Matt put on his best "interested fellow geek" face. "I'm looking for some Trek episodes…"

Frank pointed, annoyed, at the far row, where perfectly legitimate boxed DVD sets sat waiting. "Over there." He then returned to his conversation. "Anyway, as I was saying…"

Matt interrupted again. "I was really looking for 'Fragments of the Soul' and 'The Observer Effect.'" Frank blinked and looked slightly nervous. "Um… not sure I know those. Were they, uh, late-season Voyager? 'Cause I never got too into that…"

Matt lowered his voice and pretended to be very interested in a stack of manga whose contents would please anyone whose twin fetishes were squid and schoolgirls. "No. Fourth season Classic."

Frank wavered between greed and fear, and momentarily allowed fear to win. "Sorry, dude. Uh… Trek was cancelled after three seasons, you know…"

"Sure. *Here*. But elsewhere…"

The booth's owner busied himself rearranging the patternless array of discs. "Not really sure about anywhere else, man, so…"

Time to see if the trump card worked, Matt thought. "Oh. Sorry. Bob Sinderman told me you were the one to talk to…"

Frank paused in his transformation of the discs from one shape of chaos to another. "Sinderman? You know him?"

That was the test phrase. Matt took it.

"Know *her*, actually. Bobbi. A good friend of mine. She said..."

Frank relaxed. "Oh, okay. Bobbi's cool. There was this time she wore this—" His face glazed over in a moment of remembered (and probably imagined) lust. "Anyway, yeah, I can get you those, but not here." He reached below the table and drew forth a card, scribbling something on it. "Drop by here after the con. And bring cash. A lot of cash. What you want ain't cheap."

"They're original imports, right? Not any of this scanned crap?"

"Oh yeah, man. Original, mint-in-box, straight from the Bridge. Quality only."

Matt smiled. "Cool. I'll be there." Then he purchased a few random manga and the nearest DVD – something involving cheerleaders and chainsaws – and made a show of browsing several other booths, slowly, until he had worked his way back out of the dealer's room.

Matt whistled as he looked around the packed living room. "For once, a tipoff actually worked. Sinderman must have had a real hate for him to rat him out like this. Wow."

Every flat surface was stacked with video cases, DVDs, and other media. Matt twirled a small octagonal blue crystal between his fingers. "You ever see one of these, Brian?"

Brian Friedman, a young man with clipped blonde hair and a perennially serious expression, looked over at it. "Not outside of a report. Atlantean?" Brian doled out words as if he was being charged for each one.

Matt smiled. "They call the place Atlantis, but I don't think anyone's made any real connection to the myth. Just another sea-covered world, but way ahead of us on baseline tech."

Brian frowned, something he was good at doing. "No market. Just boring costume dramas. Nothing happens for a year."

"Oh, yeah, no one's in the market for their media... but this little baby," He flipped the disc and caught it. "...can probably hold a few years worth of standard Prime DVDs. Somewhere in this junk, there's probably a hacked piece of hardware to make it play to a standard PC." He tossed the disc in a Ziploc, sealed it, and wrote the date and case number on the outside. He looked for a safe place to set it down, saw none, and shoved it in his jacket pocket for the moment. "What else we got? Anything really good?"

Matt's partner shrugged. "Not much quality. Quantity. He's got contacts in two, three dozen alts. Almost all sci-fi stuff."

"Yeah, for some reason, no one wants those three seasons of Bonanza with Ronald Reagan."

"Check his system. Names, contacts, Bridge frequencies. Huh. Odd."

Matt walked over. "What?"

Brian handed him a stack of pamphlets and posters. "Fudge Hershey!" one declared. "There's Nothing Sweet About Slave Labor" decreed another.

"Looks like ol' Frank has a socially active side." Brian continued to sort through the papers.

Matt laid the pamphlets down on top of a stack of videotapes showcasing Alec Guinness as Dr. Who. "That might explain it, then. If there is some kind of political infighting in whatever fringe group he's a part of, that could have prompted the ratting-out." He laughed. "Political activists and science fiction fans… both prone to violent ideological wars over crap. And our Frankie is both."

There was a sudden thumping noise.

Brian turned to Matt. "Place was supposed to be empty.

Matt nodded. "It was… might just be some junk falling down. I'll check it out."

"Should I come along?"

"Uh… sure. I mean, it's probably a cat. It's not like alternate universe video bootleggers are known for their violent tendencies."

"Protocol."

Matt sighed. "Right. This is pathetic." He flipped open his cell phone. "Agent Matt Anders, Copyright Enforcement, reporting a disturbance at the suspect's home. Investigating." Follow the rules, fill out the forms, dot the 'i's…

The two walked through the cluttered apartment, past walls of books (including, Matt noted with a start, *all* of Hitler's sci-fi, in deluxe hardcover – worth ten grand, at least), and headed towards the stairs leading to the loft. The cops had supposedly checked out the place when they arrested Big Frank, so there shouldn't be anyone upstairs at all. Still, it was sometimes better to be a little paranoid than a lot dead.

The upstairs area was even more cluttered than the down. There was also a distinct odor, the familiar smell of the unwashed geek. Open Chinese food containers in varying degrees of independent evolution towards sapience cluttered the floor, and a bed whose stains formed a Rorschach test as done by Jackson Pollack was sitting in the middle of the room.

Matt frowned.

"That bed should have been over there. Look, the floor's a slightly lighter shade of puke brown." He glanced at the opposite wall. "So it was recently pushed against that wall, then pushed away..." He pulled it further away and looked at the wall. There was a poorly concealed doorway. "Hidden room? Wonder if our Frank is smuggling in Orion slave girls or..."

There was a sudden scuttling and thumping from the far end of the room. Matt and Brian both turned to see something, or someone, dashing out from behind a desk. They both ran to follow, Brian clearly in the lead, leaping down the stairs. Matt followed as quickly as he could, but tripped over a pile of books Brian had knocked down in his haste. As he struggled to his feet, he heard a clear "Halt!" followed by a gunshot.

Gunshot?

At first, he thought Brian had been shot. When he arrived in the front room, though, he saw Brian holding a still-smoking pistol, and a small body splayed on the floor in a growing puddle of dark blood.

"You brought a *gun* on a *copyright enforcement* check?"

Brian looked perturbed. "Standard policy. This is a crime scene. Why didn't you?"

Matt tried for a moment to wrap his mind around what seemed a truly ludicrous question, then snapped back to present reality. "Why did you shoot him? Hell, *what* did you shoot?" He moved forward to examine the body.

"Hold on. Coroner will be coming. Don't touch the body."

"How do you know it... he... whatever's... even dead? We have to..." Matt had reached the body.

It was tiny, about three feet in height, and reasonably proportioned. It was dressed in bright blue clothing, with soft boots. Nearby was a small knife. Matt reached for the wrist, and quickly noted the lack of a pulse. He carefully turned the body over; ignoring Brian's protests, and saw the shot had struck the heart. There was no hope of revival.

He looked at the dead figure for a moment. It was a man with the look of a fat person gone suddenly and painfully to thin, apparently in his late thirties, though the size of a child of seven or so. His face was gaunt and hollow, and his hands were badly scarred. His eyes were still open, staring into nothingness.

Matt slowly stepped away from the body and looked for something to wipe his hands on, then gave up. Instead, he wheeled on Brian. "You want to explain why you shot Frodo?"

Brian tried, and failed, to smile. "Not a hobbit. Shoes. Round ears. The Perp was a munchkin."

"Perp? What is he guilty of? Why the fuck did you shoot him?" Matt struggled to retain professional detachment. Copyright investigation rarely placed him face-to-face with bloody violence of any sort, and it wasn't something that sat well with him.

Brian's stoic demeanor began to fail. "He had a knife! Look!" Brian pointed at the small weapon.

"You shot someone because he had a pen-knife? For God's sake, Brian, *look* at him! He's a wreck! You could have taken him out one handed!"

"He *drew a weapon on me!*" Brian's voice cracked, and the words he normally rationed suddenly flowed with uncharacteristic speed. "What the hell else was I supposed to do? Wait for him to hurl it into my throat? It was pure self defense!"

"Did you even ask him to drop it?"

"Of… of course I did! Told him to drop it, put his hands up… he didn't respond! I had to do something!"

"I didn't hear any of that."

"You missed it, then. Look, I said it, all right? I did what I was supposed to do." He began to grow flushed.

Matt put his hands to his face, and then realized, too late, he had just smeared himself with his munchkin blood. "We're *copyright enforcement*, Brian! We don't kill people!"

"We're *law* enforcement. We do what we have to. Just… just drop it, okay? I did what I was supposed to do, that's all. Just… just drop it."

"They dropped it?"

Matt stared disbelievingly at his supervisor.

"Julius… that's just ridiculous. Brian killed a man… yes, a

man, dammit, don't give me that look... in cold blood!"

Julius Glen's mouth formed a particularly twisted expression, almost a tilde. That was his almost-patented 'I'm looking for the perfect weasel words' facial expression, and he found them quickly.

"Not quite cold blood, Matt. Call it... warm blood. I mean... the suspect was armed. It was a crime scene under active investigation. Agents have died in the field before."

Matt looked for something to break, and then remembered he was in his boss's office and restrained himself. He gave a loud grunt of frustration and began again. "It was a copyright case. And not even one involving some kind of big Asian syndicates with mob ties. This was a damn nerd with a munchkin in his closet!"

Julius nodded, with a patronizing half-smile. "Indeed. He was probably a slaver. Or running illegal immigrants. Sadly, we'll never know..."

Matt found his thoughts suddenly derailed from the outraged speech he was about to make. "Never know? Huh? We got three computers off nerd-boy. Plus, he's in custody. It's not like he won't sing loudly for any shot at a reduced sentence."

Supervisor Glen's face wavered between surprise and embarrassment. "Oh... you didn't... I mean, you were on the case, you should have received..." He turned to his computer and began scrolling through emails. "Oh. Damn. Matt, I'm sorry, but it looks like there was some kind of fuck-up. Your name got dropped from the cc list for this case. You never got the messages."

"What? What messages?"

"The suspect... Frank Brummerman... was, ah, killed in prison. Tragic, really. Some sort of knife fight..."

"Wait... he was killed in a knife fight in the nerd pen? What, did some credit card hacker whittle a data key into a shiv? Did a riot break out over whether was Kirk was better than Picard?"

Julius coughed. "There was an... administrative error. He was sent to a, ah, more secure institution."

Matt blinked a few times. "He... what? This is... this is passing beyond ridiculous. I suppose next you'll tell me we couldn't get anything off his systems."

Julius coughed again.

"Oh, I am *not* believing this."

"Hardware bomb. EMP pulse linked to a timer."

Matt nodded. Now, that part was almost believable. A lot of people with sensitive data had deadman switches on their hardware. But the rest of it put together… and, besides, the FBI's data teams were used to that sort of thing, and would have taken steps… he shook his head. He recognized where his thoughts were going, and he didn't like it. Still…

Matt waited a minute before speaking, to make sure he was sounding as calm and rational as possible.

"Julius, this could be political."

He just frowned.

"That guy, Frank… he was some sort of cross-world activist. Remember that whole Hershey thing, about two years back?"

"Yeah, Oompa-Loompa rights or something?"

"'Death By Chocolate.' That was the book Bathison wrote on it. Forced labor mining camps in the chocolate mountains, prison labor in molasses swamp… caused Congress to ram through a whole pile of feel-good, do-nothing labor laws, and we got a new division or two out of it."

"Cross-world labor relations enforcement. So? What of it?"

"Frank was heavy into that. I think, maybe, this whole case was a setup."

The supervisor rolled his eyes.

"Matt, we're domestic copyright enforcement. Nerd Patrol. That kind of cloak-and-dagger stuff doesn't happen here. You're taking a comedy of tragic blunders and turning it into… I don't know. A bad movie."

"Come *on*, Julius. You can't be quite so deskbound as to have lost all instinct for smelling a rat."

Julius Glen drummed his fingers and frowned. Matt smiled. This meant he was finally thinking seriously about it.

"Unlikely… silly, even… but… well, closure is good. I'm authorizing you to look into this… um… a bit on the sly, if you don't mind. Don't make it a top priority, but do what you can. Maybe one of his contacts knows something… see what you can find out."

Matt turned to leave, then stopped.

"You're supposed to warn me to be careful."

His boss stopped shuffling papers long enough to look up in confusion.

"What do you mean?"

"You're supposed to say, in a deep and serious tone, that if there's anything to this, powerful folks are behind it, and that I should watch myself."

He sighed again. "Just find out what you can. I think you've been doing too much undercover work. You're starting to think like them."

Matt laughed. "Yeah. Maybe. Look, I'll… see if anything obvious turns up. I've got a pretty hefty caseload as it is… I'm hoping to get a lead on whose been supplying those Stormfront bastards with films from Reich-3."

"Be good if we could crack that one. I'm tired of playing whack-a-mole with them. Good luck."

Matt nodded and walked out, closing the door quietly. He made his way back to his desk, started to sit, noticed the time, and then wandered to the small kitchen area. He fumbled among the rows of brown bags in the fridge until he found the one with a hastily scrawled 'M' on it, then returned to his desk and, after clearing a small spot in the clutter, began to eat.

The tuna salad seemed even more flavorless than usual, and the bread had absorbed a bit too much liquid and was turning to sodden mush in his hands. He didn't care.

Idly, he called up his files on the Stormfront case, but ignored the resulting stream of data. Chasing down Neo-Nazis who planned to destroy America in some fiendish terrorist plot? That would be worthwhile. Tracking down Neo-Nazis smuggling in movies and TV shows from some alternate world where the shitheads they worshipped had won, so they could sit in their musty basements and jerk-off to seeing their power fantasies fulfilled? Hardly worth bothering with, but these days, copyright law was starting to trump everything. With so much material wealth flowing in from the endless worlds out there, the one thing people needed more and more was entertainment, some way to fill the hours, and thanks to laws passed prior to the development of the Bridges, the entertainment conglomerates had incredible control over the flow of any kind of information which might even arguably qualify as media. The only thing bigger was immigration and emigration, and Matt found that even less palatable. He'd seen the faces of people being sent back to their hellworlds, pitilessly tossed into temporary Bridges to be dumped back into whatever sick disaster they were fleeing. Hmm. Immigration…

He brought up the directory. There was that one guy he knew from training… Harold? Harry? Yeah, he preferred Harry… there he was. He clicked the name, and an image blossomed on his console, a doughy man going prematurely bald and fat. He didn't seem to recognize Matt.

"Um... yeah? Harry Kravik. Immigration. Can I help you?"

Matt struggle to force joviality into his voice "Hey! Matt here, Matt Anders? We were in handgun training together, back at the Academy?"

"Uh... Yeah, oh yeah, I remember you..." said Harry, who very obviously didn't. "What can I do for you," he added, with the fairly obvious coda that it had better be something extremely trivial.

"Just looking for an opinion... do we have a lot of immigration issues with Oz?"

Harry's face fluttered, as he tried to draw out the answer to the question from his brain without having to perform any actual work. "Which one? We got, ah, the one which was nuked back in '64, the one which got hit by that tsunami, the one which is still a penal colony..."

Matt shook his head. "Not Australia. Oz. The merry-old-land-of."

Harry smiled and laughed. "That place? Oh, hell no. *Emigration*, sure, got way too many people want to play around in fairy-land, but there's hardly anyone who wants to leave. I mean, only that Dorothy chick would be stupid enough to want to go back to Kansas, right?"

"So, there'd be no money in Bridgerunning to there, at least not coming our way? Not something someone would do on the side to pick up some spare bucks... or doubloons, or gold pieces, or whatever they use for cash there?"

Harry shook his head. "No way there'd be enough traffic to be worth the risk. I mean, maybe some witch fleeing an executioner with a bucket, but that's about it... Why?"

"Just... clearing out some old case files." Please, Matt thought, be lazy and unconcerned. Be lazy and unconcerned.

Harry pondered this for about a second, then seemed to find the non-answer perfectly satisfying. "Oh. Okay. Uh, glad I could help out an old friend from training. We should do lunch sometime."

"Yeah. Sometime. Thanks!" Matt cut the connection.

Strike one, he thought. Frank wasn't just smuggling in munchkins en masse. That meant twinkle-toes was here for some kind of purpose.

Furthermore, Julius Glen was almost certainly part of it.

Matt sighed. Am I spinning this too much? Now I've got the 'corrupt boss who reveals himself in the shocking twist' tacked on to my growing delusion. Still... he was too blasé. He wouldn't tolerate that string of blunders happening on his watch unless he was sure he'd be protected from any kind of retribution. Everyone was just being too damn forgiving, too willing to shrug and say 'tragic human error.' The FBI wasn't about being forgiving.

How paranoid should I be, he wondered? How far will Glen go? Is this big enough to risk killing me over?

I don't know, he realized. And unless I investigate more, I won't know – and investigating more is likely to be put me more at risk. Damn.

He reached for his console again, and then paused. He flipped open his briefcase and took out a small personal computer, one he carried with him for traffic jams or purely personal use. Then he gathered up all of his work thus far on the Frank case, placed it in a special directory, and touched the keyboard with his index finger. A light on the keyboard flashed briefly red, then went green. He then transferred the data over to his personal system, logged it into a few places, and signed off. He contemplated wiping the data from the finger chip, as well, but decided he might need it again.

Now where to?

He brought the Frank data up again, and filtered back through the history. He had only one real lead: the woman who'd betrayed him.

Roberta Sinderman's face shone a ghostly, eerie, blue. This was due to neither makeup nor mutation, but the fact that her apartment was lit entirely by computer screens, ranging from some ancient cathode tubes to the latest free-space displays. Her hands moved deftly from one input device to another, as if she was playing a half-dozen organs at once, conducting a symphony of information which flickered in pulses of light from one screen to another.

Then, just as the final movement was nearing its crescendo, the performance was interrupted by the insistent intrusion of the technology of the 19th Century – the telephone. Bobbi sent forth a long string of profanity in several languages, some of which were not native to Earth. Around her, patterns of data clashed discordantly: conversational queries hung unanswered as game avatars succumbed to violent attacks, while stacks of paper and assorted gewgaws went flying, detritus hurled aside in the frantic search for the phone.

By the time she found it, on the sixth ring, fury and frustration had peaked. She flipped it open and snarled. “Someone better be dying.”

The voice on the other side paused for a moment, taken aback, then replied: “Someone is. Dead, actually. We need to talk.”

There was a Starbucks nearby. There always was. Rumor had it a certain class of rich would-be émigrés were paying illicit Bridgerunners a fortune for access to any 1-Delta parallel which lacked Starbucks. To date, none had been officially found, but many of the wealthy and gullible had paid real money for false coordinates.

Bobbi and Matt sat at a small table, surrounded by unkempt college students and young businessmen. The din of the crowd (not to mention the complete self-absorption of those who composed it) provided near perfect privacy.

Matt sipped his coffee, frowned, and added more ‘Perfection,’ the latest trend in non-fattening sweeteners. It was sugar, really; it just had some sort of molecular twist that rendered it indigestible. Another commoditized miracle, courtesy of the Bridges.

Bobbi poked listlessly at her pie as her coffee sublimated from ‘volcanic’ to ‘glacial’ while completely skipping ‘pleasantly hot.’ She tried to find something witty or insightful to say, and failed utterly.

“Frank’s really dead?”

Images of a dead munchkin dancing in his mind, Matt fought back the impulse to say “really most sincerely dead,” and instead just said, “Yes. Toss someone like that into a maximum-security prison, he was pretty much certain to be. Especially if someone *wanted* him to be.” He paused, sipped, and continued. “Did you want him dead, Ms. Sinderman?”

“Just... just call me Bobbi. And, no, no, of course I didn’t want the stupid fat bastard dead!” Her voice was rising to the point where the unspoken rules of polite ignorance were being strained. One or two of the most extremely bored glanced over at them. She dropped back to a polite whisper.

“But you turned him in.” It was a statement, not a question.

“Yes. Yes, I did, but only... I mean, I wanted him to suffer a little, maybe scare the crap out of him when the feds showed up at his door... but, even today, you don't get *killed* for copyright violation. I'm pretty sure Congress rejected that amendment to the Bono Act..."

Matt tried to resist smiling, and failed. "Actually, it passed, but the Supreme Court overturned it 5-4. This is... something else. I think. I don't think it had anything to do with the copyrights. Would... would anyone else have a reason to want him dead?"

Bobbi laughed. "Only everyone who knew him, at one point or another. He was a leech, a letch, a braggart, greedy, selfish, ill-mannered... he'd probably pissed off every friend he had over the years."

"Any of them have the kind of pull and connections needed to arrange for him to get killed?"

She shook her head. "No... maybe someone with incredible hacking skills might have gotten into the FBI's systems... but just for that? The guys I know who could do that wouldn't waste their time offing Frank. They'd wipe all your records or free everyone arrested for pot smoking or just send snarky emails to every agent on the system, just to show they'd done it. Frank was a jerk, but you don't kill someone for being a jerk." She paused. "At least not among science fiction fans. There'd be no one left."

Matt took out some of the photos he'd downloaded from the case file and printed out. They showed the sprawled, bloody, body of the dead munchkin. "Do you know this man?"

Bobbi looked at the images, flipping slowly between them. She cycled the entire stack four times before she answered. "No. No idea. The... the books and tapes next to the body... was this a kid?"

"No. A Munchkin."

Bobbi snorted, then blushed. "Oh God... I shouldn't laugh... I shouldn't... but... a dead munchkin? In Frank's house? First those Oompa-Loompas, now..." She took a sip of the now-glacial coffee. "He always did take things too far. It always amazed me how someone who could be such a total jerk in so many ways still took risks to help people. I think it was some sort of ego thing, like if he helped enough strangers it made up for being an asshole to his actual friends.

"So what was he saving the munchkins from?"

"I don't know. I was hoping you could tell me."

"No... maybe. I need to check my files. He might have sent me something that I ignored." She looked at the coffee, which was now beginning to congeal. "Let's get back to my place for a bit. I might be able to help you."

Upon reflection, Matt realized he'd spent much less time in single women's apartments than he would have liked, but even given the lack of data points, he knew Bobbi's was on the far end of the bell curve. Much like Frank's, every flat area seemingly had something on it, but Bobbi was a lot more eclectic than Frank. A lot nicer to look at, too, shouted his hindbrain, but he ignored it as best he could, which wasn't very well. She certainly wasn't cover girl material, with her black hair done up in a hasty ponytail, her mostly-shapeless jeans and sweatshirt trying and almost succeeding in disguising her figure, and her passionate lack of makeup, but there was an unadorned attractiveness there which he found hard to ignore. Not that the situation was exactly conducive to romance – "Hi, I'm here to discuss the guy you might have gotten killed," wasn't one of the world-class pickup lines. He shunted any random thoughts of romance back to the cellars of his mind and put on his best professionally neutral expression.

"So... what is it you do, exactly? For a living, I mean?"

Bobbi paused for a moment in her frantic tapping. "Conversion filters, mostly. Bringing stuff from one format to another. *Legitimate* data, by the way. All licensed appropriately. Over-the-Bridge corps don't want to change their files, our corps don't want to change theirs, so I write the tools which help them join up to exploit infinity together. That's how Frank and I met, actually. He needed my skills... and since he needed something, he was actually passing for a pretty nice guy."

She stopped working, and then drummed her fingers. "Really nothing useful here. I... hum. You know, Tim might know."

"Tim?"

"Yeah. He... well... he's sort of the guy who started this whole mess. Sort of a friend. Hanger on, really. A little creepy, a little weird... but no more so than most of the folks I hang with." Bobbi looked momentarily embarrassed – a state that Matt sensed was unusual for her. "Anyway, as of a few weeks ago, we... that is, Frank and I... we were, well..."

"An item?" Matt volunteered.

Bobbi smiled at the horridly polite euphemism. "Yeah. An item. But Frank..."

"Wasn't exactly inclined to monogamy, and, let me guess, Tim was the one who pointed this out to you."

"Good guess. I'm not sure if he was looking to get into my pants himself, or was just one of the many people with a hate-on for Frank, or both. So, yeah, he told me. Then..."

She stopped to think.

"Then, we were both a little drunk... Okay, I was kind of a lot drunk... and he was talking about ways I could get back at him, all sorts of stupid, wacky, shit, like hacking all his files, or posting some nasty forgeries to the net, or building some sort of paint bomb or the like to embarrass the crap out of him, and then one of us... I think it was him, I don't know, it might have been me... said to just tip off you guys. He'd wet himself if the feds came to his door. We figured... I figured, I guess, that he'd plea bargain, a couple of months community service picking up trash or delivering meals to old ladies or something. I mean, you don't... you don't get *killed* for pirating Star Trek!" There was sudden emotion to her voice. She looked back at Matt. "I got him killed, didn't I? I'm responsible. I killed... I mean, he was a bastard and a creep and I wanted him to pay, but... this is just..."

She took a moment to gather herself. "I'm sorry. It's just all... sinking in. I got a man killed. That's... a lot."

Two men, Matt thought, but figured it was impolitic to say as much. She seemed to be suffering enough guilt right now, more than she deserved.

"Look, really, it's not your fault. What happened was not something anyone could have expected."

"I suppose... hey!" She slapped her head. "Tim! He's the one who pointed out the shit Frank was pulling, he might have some idea why he was hiding a munchkin!"

Matt tried not to smile. *Hiding a munchkin* sure sounded like a euphemism for something, though he wasn't sure what.

"Yes... good idea. Maybe he can help."

"He lives a few blocks from here. Let's go see if he's home."

"Shouldn't we call?" Matt said, as Bobbi began performing a complex ritual of setting her multiple systems into various modes of standby or rest.

"Nah. He's one of those people who never takes calls. Best to surprise him."

Tim lived in a neighborhood that was just on the right side of gentrification – plenty of interesting and unique local businesses still open, but most of the homeless had been swept to other, less fortunate, locales. His apartment was in a walk-up loft. Bobbi timed her entrance to follow a different resident through the gate, avoiding the problem of calling up for entry. He was on the third floor, and Matt found himself right on the edge of winded after climbing the stairs.

She knocked on the door, then listened at it, then knocked harder. "Dammit, Tim, I know you're in there! Open up, we've gotta talk. It's about Frank..."

She had barely finished the name when the door surged open.

"Tim, I..." she began, but Matt interrupted her.

"*Brian?*" he shouted, incredulous.

"*Matt?*" came the reply.

"Tim? Brian? What?" was all Bobbi could manage.

"Shit!" said Matt and Brian simultaneously. Then Matt raised the ante by shoving Brian/Tim backwards through the door.

Brian staggered, but remained standing. His face attempted to find an expression other than its usual mild frown, but failed. "Matt. Stop. Think a moment. You do not want to be involved in this. Go home now."

Matt continued to advance. "You're a piece of work, aren't you? How deep are you in this? For that matter, what *is* this? What the *hell* is going on exactly?" Brian kept trying to stay out of his way, kept backing up, towards...

"Oh no... not this time!" Matt leaped for the gun on the table, trying to keep it away from Brian. Bobbi, meanwhile, was staring at the developing fight in confusion. "Wait... you guys know each other?" Pieces fell together. "You set me up, you bastard!" She wheeled on Brian and began to pummel him, vigorously if somewhat futilely. "You..."

He hit her, twice, once in the stomach and then in the head. She fell back, coughing. "Yes." He seemed almost bored with it, and relieved he could drop the pretense. "Yes, I used you. We wanted the tip-off to come from outside. Your involvement should have ended there. This whole matter is supposed to be over with!"

"You wanna bet?" Matt had taken advantage of Bobbi's otherwise ineffectual attack to grab the gun. "I think we're all going to have a very long chat."

Brian finally managed to smile. "You're not going to shoot me."

"You wanna bet?" Matt tightened his grip and took careful aim. "I figure you're guilty of at least murder, plus God knows what else. I'd prefer to take you in, but if you think I'd hesitate to kill you, you're wrong. Why wouldn't I shoot?"

"It's not loaded." Brian said. Then he leapt for Matt.

Matt fired, and was rewarded with a hollow click. He had barely enough time to register this before Brian was on him.

Brian was stronger and better trained. He casually knocked the gun from Matt's hand, and then began seriously pummeling his partner. Oddly, he refrained from talking. As Matt staggered from one punch after another, and began tasting blood and see his vision blur, he found himself thinking: *The least he could do is gloat. Or explain what's going on. A monologue would be nice now. Don't the bad guys* gloat *any more?*

There was a sudden breaking sound. Matt thought, at first, that it was something internal, but then he realized nothing inside him was made of porcelain. Brian stood, momentarily staggered, soaking wet, and covered with small red flowers.

Matt punched him as hard as he could. He fell back, looked at Matt, tried to recover his balance, and then tumbled through the window.

Matt and Bobbi rushed to the halo of shattered glass. Brian had managed to pass through a stubby tree, which had cushioned his fall somewhat. The figure on the sidewalk, though twisted like a broken marionette and surrounded by an artistic halo of blood, seemed to be alive. A crowd gathered, and fingers, eyes, and angry voices aimed upwards at the shattered window and the pair silhouetted within.

Matt stepped back from the window, and then pulled at a stunned Bobbi, "You've been here before. Is there a way out? Other than the front, I mean?"

Bobbi kept staring at the shattered glass.

"Look, I hate to wallow in melodrama here, but I've got a feeling we need to get away, fast. Please! Both of our lives…"

"The garage door."

"Huh?"

"Yeah. There's a back door. Ti… Bri… whatever the hell his name was always left using the basement garage." She slowly came out of her haze and looked around. "There. His keys."

Matt raced to the door, grabbing the keys from the table as he did. Something else caught his eye. There was a small stack of bills there… sort of. They were too large, and the color was a very faded and dull green, almost muddy. Modern money had adapted dozens of anti-counterfeiting measures. This was just very boring paper, except for having the wrong presidents on it. William Jennings Bryan? *Maybe it's a clue*, Matt thought. He pocketed the bills, then glanced back at Bobbi. "You know which car is his?"

"Yeah. He… Hey, did you just rob him? What, fascist for hire doesn't pay well enough?"

Matt gaped at her. Her mind went to the strangest places at the worst times. "This might be important. Crossworld currency smuggling? Maybe that's what this is all about. Now, the car?"

Bobbi shook herself back to the present moment. "Right, car. It was this red thing, it…" she paused again, as another round of emotion besieged her self control. Matt grabbed her arm.

"Just point it out to me. Come *on!*"

Brian's car was a Bridge-imported 2004 Stanley Steamer. A bumper sticker read "Preserve The Prime." Matt wondered, for a moment, if this reflected some unknown environmental idealism on Brian's part, or if the steamer was simply part of creating a cover identity. *I'll probably never know,* he realized, and got into the driver's seat. Bobbi got in as well.

The vehicle started up instantly, the technology of its homeworld having long since solved the various problems of steam-powered vehicles. Lightweight materials and advances in steam engine technology and heat recycling enabled them to compete with gas engines for performance, though the Bridge transfer costs were prohibitive. They, like the old hybrids which were popular before the Bridges made 'the end of oil' as meaningless a phrase as 'too old to rock and roll,' were driven mostly by the smug and wealthy, who didn't object to paying a bit extra for the chance to help the environment in a very public way.

The controls were close enough to normal cars that Matt quickly got the craft moving out of the garage and onto the streets, where he set off in a random direction, even as sirens began to wail in the background.

After a minute, Bobbi spoke.

"Why are we running? You're an FBI agent! Why don't you just talk to the cops?"

Matt turned onto the highway.

"Because this is something that reaches far up the Agency's ladder, and I don't know what it is or have any kind of evidence yet.

So my story is just that – a story – and it's pretty likely whoever is in charge will make sure I'm held for attempted murder, and, if you're lucky, you too."

"And if I'm unlucky?"

"You'll be cleared of all charges, or be allowed to plea-bargain your way down to nothing, and then you'll have some sort of tragic accident."

"Oh." Then. "Oh! So what do we do?"

"We're still where we were. We need to know what the hell's going on, and how it involves a munchkin in someone's closet! God, every time I say that, it sounds ridiculous." He reached up to tap his right eye, now becoming nicely swollen. "But it's all real."

Bobbi sat up suddenly. "Take exit 12."

Matt veered over, serenaded by a chorus of angry horns and squealing tires, bouncing onto the off ramp with inches to spare. "Now where?"

"Left... straight three blocks... right."

"Where are we going?"

"With a little luck... Oz."

The warehouse could only be described as nondescript, but the cars parked in front of it were anything but. All were decorated with various stickers and decals informing passersby of the owner's political, social, and economic views, which seemed to vary from radical communism to hardcore libertarianism with no stop anywhere on the political spectrum that might garner actual votes. One car managed to sport both IWW (recently renamed the WIW, for Workers of Infinite Worlds) and NRA bumper stickers. Matt just shrugged.

"Why are we—" he began.

"Take off that suit. Or at least the jacket. And hide the badge. Try not to look like a narc."

Matt blinked. "We're running from the police and you're stopping to score drugs? Bobbi, are you..."

She sighed and rolled her eyes. "Not drugs! This is... oh, just come inside."

The inside of the warehouse was a mad tangle of technology. Bright lights shone down from above, illuminating every corner.

Matt wandered, momentarily awestruck, through what could pass as the attic of some museum of the history of science. Everywhere there were wonders; and everywhere those wonders were in various states of disrepair. He stopped and stared at one machine in particular, a 15 foot tall, 30 foot long monstrosity that spewed steam and stank of oil. It was composed it seemed, of tens of thousands of gears no more than a half-inch across...

"A Babbage Fin De Siecle!" said a high-pitched, but still male, voice. "Fully functional, too!"

There was a derisive snort. "Yeah, if by 'fully functional,' you mean 'breaks down twice a week.'"

A high-pitched-voice responded. "So, did that *laufpanzer* of yours manage to go three steps yet?"

Snorter continued the intellectual debate. "It could crush that tinker toy!"

"By falling on it, maybe. Which is all you've managed to get it to do."

Bobbi looked pained. "Guys, a little help, here? Is Karen around?"

"Yeah. Over in the back, of course."

Matt managed to get a glimpse at the two verbal combatants. One was tall and gawky, pushing six feet, and moved as if he had his brain recently implanted in a new body and wasn't sure how to use it properly. He had a mass of curly hair and a shirt pocket full of small wrenches and other, less identifiable, tools. His partner-in-debate was five feet tall and nearly as wide, wearing a t-shirt that might once have been black but which was now torn, stained, faded, and full of more holes than Bonnie and Clyde's car. He also wielded a wrench that could easily have brained a small elephant.

Bobbi grabbed Matt's hand, pulling him away from his study of the ornate gearwork and the debating technophiles. "This way."

The two made their way through a maze of bizarre machines and obsessive individuals tinkering with them. Matt noted that nearly everything seemed to be, well, low tech. He was used to smugglers bringing in everything from light sabers to bioengineered slaves, but he knew of no market for a mechanical version of Space Invaders or what looked like a strange cross between a telegraph and a fax machine.

As the two reached the back, they walked into two people having an argument, one of those arguments which, it seemed, they'd had a dozen times before. It was almost scripted.

A woman with grey streaked hair, sharp black eyes, and a light southern accent was speaking her part. "...infinite possibilities doesn't make sense. The odds are too high. Y'all'd be lucky to find one fictive, not the dozens we've charted."

Her longtime opponent was a round, balding, man wearing a t-shirt covered with complex physics. Matt suspected they might be the Bridge equations. "Any idea of vibrational inspiration is a metaphysical nightmare. Look. Suppose the Fox Theorem is right. Suppose that the reason we can find worlds out of fiction is because, somehow, writers 'tuned into' them and were inspired. Think what that means. Entire universes might exist for no reason than to host some long-forgotten romance novel. Hell, our own world could just be words on a screen..."

"I pity the poor writer who'd go and try it. Who would have believed it? In the Mid-80s, a physics student is playing around with field equations, transposes a few variables, and, poof! All of infinity opens up for dirt-cheap. It's a crappy premise for a novel. Some fella once said 'Fiction is harder to write than non-fiction 'cause fiction must be believable.' But you never mind that. You're using argument from consequence... you don't like where the theory leads, so you..." She looked up, finally noticing her two visitors.

"Uh... sorry. Hey, Bobbi! How goes? Who's your, uh, friend?"

"This is Matt. Matt, Karen Devernais."

"Call me Katie," she said as she took his outstretched hand. She shook it warmly, and then looked suspiciously at Bobbi. "Is he cool?"

Bobbi quickly weighed the precise degree of truth she felt she could get away with, and decided it was very small. "Him? Oh, yeah, don't mind the monkey suit. He's got a crap job. Anyway, he's a friend of Tim's."

The balding man looked up. "Huh. How *is* Tim, anyway? He's been even quieter than usual lately..."

Bobbi wished, for an instant, that she had the sort of wit that would come up with a wonderful double-entendre that somehow involved defenestration. Sadly, she realized grimly, she didn't. "He's fine. A bit busy."

"Yeah, but he told me he might drop in soon," said Matt with a barely controlled smirk. Bobbi glared at him. It was patently unfair that he got to make the obvious joke. *I'm supposed to be the snarky one*, she thought. He's the square who finally loosens up. She rubbed her stomach, still sore from Brian's punch. And this *isn't* some sort of buddy comedy.

"So… what can I do for y'all?" Katie asked.

Bobbi hunkered down next to her, after clearing away a small pile of electromechanical debris. "We need to *go somewhere*."

Karen looked back at her. "Why not just say 'wink, wink'? Bobbi, you were always about as subtle as a hand grenade in an outhouse."

Matt quickly added up the numbers. "You've got a Bridge here? *Here?*"

"Yeeeesss… um… Bobbi… you know, if you need to impress some guy you just met, *maybe* bringing him to a club where not-entirely-legal things go on *isn't the best idea*?"

Matt's feeling of being nonplussed deepened. "Um… I'm standing right here."

Katie glanced over at him and conveyed, with a quick and perfect glance, that she was both completely aware of, and completely unconcerned with, that fact.

"Katie, look, we…" Bobbi glanced at the balding man.

"Chuck, if you don't mind…"

"Fine, whatever. I'll just go tighten some lug nuts or something…" He wandered off, mumbling some mild imprecations under his breath.

Katie smiled. "They need Bridges for their little projects, I provide them, I get to make the rules. Now, what's up?"

Bobbi glanced over at Matt. Matt just nodded.

Bobbi told her.

Katie listened. Then she stood up, walked two steps in one direction, turned, walked a few steps in another direction, stopped, then returned to her seat and said nothing for a minute. Then she spoke.

"Munchkins. Dead munchkins."

"Only one so far," Matt noted. "But there may be more. We don't know. We need to find out."

Katie considered. "And you won't mention this little club to any of your fascist friends?"

Matt decided not to point out that Brian/Tim already knew and would have told anyone if it mattered. "If I have any friends – fascist or otherwise – left after this debacle, I won't say anything. You're… um… not importing slaves or spice or that porno movie featuring Richard Nixon, are you?"

"'Tricky Dick Does DC?' No, nothing like that. This is the Bridge Anachronistic Technological Society."

Matt pondered that for a second. "BATS? Spent a lot of time on that acronym?"

"Not really, no."

"Anachronistic tech?"

"You know. Difference engines. Nazi mecha. Japanese steam powered dirigible fortresses. Da Vinci ornithopters. Half of it can't work here at all, and none of it's really useful or practical. It's just *cool*. But a lot of it's technically military hardware, so..."

"Never mind, I get it. Can you get us to Oz?"

"Sure thing. The coordinates for Emerald City Tourism Board are well doc'ed. Type 'em in, and off you go. Word of warning... if you even think about trying to swipe a piece of the road as a 'souvenir,' you will be shipped off to the Nome King's emerald mines. They're pretty strict about that."

Bobbi leapt up. "Great! We go, you do your FBI sleuthing stuff, you solve the case, you get a medal, and I get my life back." She had a momentary thought. "Speaking of which..."

She took out a cell phone and tapped some keys. A glowing holographic field expanded out from it. She began putting in a sequence. "Just wanted to check my apartment security... got a minicam overlooking... *shit!*"

Matt saw it. A squad of police was busily tearing through Bobbi's apartment, showing all of their usual care and concern for other people's property. She screamed and hurled imprecations and insults as they professionally desecrated countless items of valuable trivia. Within a minute, she had been reduced to sputtering profanity in between sobs of anger and frustration. Matt and Katie both attempted to calm her.

"Look, look, Bobbi, please, we'll get the fuckers, really; you just got to focus here...."

"She's right. This is why we came. Once this is cleared up, we can..."

"What? Just put my whole damn life back together? This is... this is all just *nuts*, I mean, I got up this morning expecting the worst thing that would happen to me is getting fragged in some game, and now... now... I mean, shit, you're used to this! This is your job!"

Matt stepped back. "Uh... no, my job is mostly filing reports on people who like TV too much. The first time I saw a man killed was back in Frank's house…" He paused. Something clicked. He began rummaging through his jacket. "Aha!"

He pulled out a Ziploc bag with a blue octagon in it. Bobbi stared at it.

"What the…?"

Katie's eyes widened. "Atlantean. Shoot, haven't seen much of that around. Where'd you find it?"

"Frank's place."

Bobbi blinked. "Two weeks ago?"

"When that whole mess with the munchkin happened, I forgot about it…"

"Yeah, but… it was in your jacket for two weeks? Don't you *wash* that thing?" She backed away in mock horror. "They picked the right guy for geek patrol." She began to laugh, her mood swinging violently away from the frustration of moments before. Matt looked wounded.

"I only *wear* this when I'm on field assignment. Which isn't often."

"I'm sorry," She kept laughing. "I know it's… it's just… hell, I needed to laugh…"

Katie was tapping her foot. "Can we get on with this? I've got an illegal interdimensional nexus to run."

Bobbi choked back both her laughter and tears. "I'm sorry, Katie. Sure. Oz, please."

Matt shook his head. "No." He took in their stunned and confused expressions, and then began to speak just as it looked as if they were going to begin verbally scouring him. "It's not going to be at the main portal. Whatever's going on, it's not happening where there's a lot of official inter-world action. It's going to be at some other Bridge point."

Karen gritted her teeth. "Well, that's just dandy. It's not like I can just magically dump you right where you might need to be. Without the right numbers, you'll end up in the Deadly Desert or even worse… depression era Kansas."

Matt tossed her the blue octagon.

"It will be on there. I'm sure of it."

"We can hack up some kind of reader, I guess… but figuring out the data…"

Bobbi sighed. "Is what I get paid the big bucks for. Let's get to work."

Watching computer geeks, well, geeking, was, Matt realized,

stunningly dull. So, he discovered, was hearing people discuss, with a passion normally reserved for sex or sports, the intricate gearwork of Victorian computers or precisely how the concept of 'armor plated zeppelin' was not utterly oxymoronic. So it was with great relief when a victory howl emerged from behind banks of monitors.

He dashed over to them. "Did you get it?"

Katie smiled. "Got it." Then her expression darkened. "Thing is… I'm not all that sure where you'll end up. We've got the spot, but it's not like I can easily map it. You're going to have to trust these numbers…"

"I don't think we have much choice."

"Well then!" Katie stood up and began walking towards what appeared to be one more pile of random mechanical components. "Here she is! My very own homemade Bridge generator! I call her 'Darlene.'" She then winked at Bobbi, enjoying Matt's rather obvious discomfiture. She began keying the coordinates in, using an antique-looking keyboard bearing a prominent "EMERAC" label. As she finished, the arcane tangle began to emit a low and uneven hum.

"Homemade? I figured you…"

"Bought a legit one on the black market? Where would the fun be in that?"

Matt stared dubiously at the tangle of wires and metal. There, in the center, was the inversion plate, and he recognized the zero-point focusing array… but it otherwise looked nothing like any Bridge he'd seen before. Bobbi leapt onto the plate happily, but he hesitated.

Katie rolled her eyes. "Oh, trust me, will ya? Look around! This whole damn warehouse is filled with crap we got over this Bridge." A sudden explosion, a shower of sparks, and a stream of profanity emerged from somewhere far back in the technological chaos. Katie flushed, and then recovered. "That was broken when we got it. Whatever it was. Now… hold it…"

There was more noise, not of explosions this time. Demands for surrender, announcements, orders…

"The cops!"

Matt looked beyond the wall of machinery. There was considerable confusion. He saw flashes of blue uniforms, then heard a horrible, wrenching sound. Something large and bronze colored was unfolding itself, rising to its massive feet. It towered over most of the rest of the junk, a vaguely humanoid collection of gears, heavily armored, and sprouting an assortment of whirling blades and vibrating knives from just about every point on its body.

Katie was momentarily distracted from her work. "Huh. So that's what that does."

Matt stared at it. "What is it?"

"Some kind of war machine, I'd guess. The spiky bits are a clue. Jerry found it, hauled it back for parts. Never could quite get it to work. I guess the gunfire woke it up. Wow. Y'know, most things like that just don't work over here, but it seems to be..."

There was the sparking of bullets on metal, as the police opened fire. It began to tromp slowly towards them. Katie kept watching. "Oh, this is gonna be a real bitch to explain..."

Matt turned to her. "Um... the Bridge?"

"Wha? Oh, right, right. Sorry. Just always wondered what that... anyway... it'll buy us a few minutes. Now, let me see here... I think this should work..."

Bobbi vanished. Matt gaped at the empty plate.

Katie smiled. "Yup, works. Now you."

"Are you sure... I mean..."

There was a sudden, horrible, noise, as if the twenty-foot colossus of bronze and iron and glass had broken some vital mainspring and collapsed into an immobile pile of metal and spikes.

"Sure I'm sure. We're goin' down, here, and you're the only chance we have." She practically shoved him onto the plate.

"You better find what you're looking for over there, 'cause I'm gonna need your story to get my ass out of jail." Then she gave him a shove and pulled a lever, even as a blue-suited policeman leapt over the barricade and grabbed at the controls. Matt saw his hand crashing down on the keyboard, saw Katie struggling to block him...

The world changed.

Sunlight replaced flickering fluorescents; trees replaced walls. There was no sensation of movement at all, just a sudden flush as temperature and pressure changed instantly. Matt looked around.

"So that's what it feels like. Huh."

He received no reply. Bobbi wasn't there.

He drew in a breath to shout, then thought better of it. Did he want to alert whoever... whatever... might be here?

The glade was calm and cool. The trees seemed normal enough, though he couldn't quite place the species. Then again, he realized, he wouldn't know an oak from a maple anyway. Birds chattered noisily at him. A squirrel glanced at him quizzically.

Matt looked back. He was slightly afraid to move; the sudden shift in perspective had given him a small touch of nausea, and he was waiting for his inner ear to adjust. The squirrel watched him, then spoke.

"You lookin' at me?"

Matt just blinked.

The squirrel cocked its head. "Huh. You a non-talkin' human? Kinda mean they dressed you up, then. You someone's pet, boy? You lost? Huh? Maybe there's a reward for you?" The squirrel's voice, which had been strangely gruff for such a tiny creature, had suddenly pitched a few octaves higher and was now a kind of childish sing-song. It leaped from the branch to alight on Matt's shoulder, and began pulling at his suit collar.

"You got a tag? You got a tag, boy? Let me see the tag, then I'll find your master for you. You'd like that, won't you boy?"

Matt's surprise finally broke. "What the hell are you talking about?"

The squirrel stopped looking for the nonexistent tag.

"Oh… you can talk. Well, nuts. Or rather, no nuts. 'Cause you probably ain't worth nothin', then."

"Wait… *you're* surprised that *I* can talk?"

The squirrel shrugged. Matt didn't know they could do that. "Well, yeah, y'know, not every animal can… I thought maybe you were someone's pet, lost in the woods. I mean, you're dressed up kinda weird…" Matt glanced down at his suit. He suddenly realized he had no idea what Oz fashions were like.

"I am no one's pet."

"Fine, whatever, can't blame a guy fer tryin'." The squirrel finally departed Matt's shoulder. "So you're a wizard, then?"

"Why would I be… oh. The suddenly appearing."

The squirrel nodded. Matt wasn't sure – the tiny furry face was very hard to read emotions on – but he thought he saw hints of frustrated exasperation there.

"No, not a wizard… I…" Matt paused. What did a squirrel know about Bridges? The Emerald City tourist link was pretty open, but this was somewhere in the boonies. I need to lie, he thought. Quickly.

"Um… a wizard… um… was angered at me and sent me away."

"Couldn't have been too angry with you, what with you still being alive and man-shaped. Hey… were you always a man? Maybe you were a fish? You kind of have that weird fish stare…" The squirrel did its best impression of a fish.

"Yes, I've always been a man! Look, I need some help…"

"Or maybe you just *think* you've always been a man! Wizards are tricky… and mostly waterproof. Hm. Are you afraid of sharks?"

"Isn't everyone?"

"Huh. Yeah, that's a lousy test." The squirrel began to think of a more comprehensive way of proving prior fishhood.

"Look, I just need… I need…"

What? The sudden paucity of his planning hit Matt, hard.

"I need to find a friend."

"So, what, now I'm your enemy?"

"No! I mean… a specific friend. She… she should be near here…"

What *did* the cop do the controls? He could be fifty feet from where Bobbi landed… or fifty miles… or… how big *was* Oz, anyway? What would Bobbi do if they were separated, where would she go?

Somewhere with technology, he reasoned. Or a Bridge home… she might head to the one place they both knew for sure had a working, two-way Bridge…

"I need to see the Wizard." Matt said, feeling smug.

"What, the one who zapped you? Why?"

"No, I mean… *the* Wizard."

"Look, Fish-Man… there's gotta be about a thousand bonded wizards… got anyone particular in mind?"

"Doesn't the Wizard rule Oz from the Emerald City?"

The squirrel blinked three times, then began to laugh, staying on the branch only by sheer animal instinct.

"You're one old fish, ain't ya? That's history book stuff! Oh, whoever zapped you's got a mean sense of humor. I'd like to meet 'im."

Matt resisted the urge to strangle the only being who offered even the vaguest hope of a lifeline. "Fine. Just… just tell me how to get to the Emerald City."

"Well, you follow the…"

"Enough! I know that part! How do I *get* to the damn road?"

"I was tryin' to tell you, Fish-Man! But if you're gonna be an asshole about it…"

"No, no, I… I'm sorry. It's just… hard… getting used to life on land."

That seemed to mollify the squirrel.

"Yeah, I get that. Okay. Like I was tryin' to say before… follow the hill down, until you come to the river… then go upstream. You'll hit a road, there, then you can probably hitch a lift to a town and take a train. By the way, you got any nuts?"

Matt made a futile show of patting his pockets. "No… sorry."

"Figures. Well, nice to meet you, Fish-Man. Mind the monkeys."

The squirrel, apparently now bored, scampered into the canopy and vanished. Matt glanced down the slope he was supposed to follow.

Monkeys?

Bobbi opened her eyes. Bridging with your eyes open was a good way to lose your lunch. Everyone knew that.

Trees. Well, that was to be expected. They looked mostly normal. She tapped at one, experimentally. It felt reasonably solid and woody.

Not sure what I was expecting, she thought. Licorice trees? I suppose I should have read the books…

She stepped away. Matt would be through in a second, and while there were all sorts of safety measures in place, she wasn't nearly as sure about the BATS' technology as she'd let on. Once the big idiot showed up, he could blunder and bully his way through this mess, shooting at things, until some kind of order was restored and her life, as she preferred it, was back on its usual track. This would all make a killer blog entry. *Fifty thousand diggs, here I come!*

A minute passed. Another. And another.

She reached for her cell phone, and then stopped, shaking her head. *Idiot! You don't have his number.*

Then: Double idiot! You think there's service in Oz?

How do you know there isn't? She said to herself.

With a smile of sudden optimism, she flipped it open.

There was no signal.

Idly, she snapped a few pictures of the tiny glade she was in. Then she tapped her foot and paced. She sat down and tried to play a game, then stopped and put the cell phone back, then stood and paced the glade again. She checked the time. Ten minutes. No Matt.

The cops, the firing… maybe he didn't make it through?

Great. This day was getting worse, a possibility she hadn't previously considered.

She considered her options. I am, I presume, in Oz. Not that I've seen anything particularly unearthly, but if I'm in the wrong world, that's just too much. And it looks like, one way or another, I'm on my own. Like that's so unusual. You'd think someone like Captain Squarejaw would be more reliable, at least. Well, fine. There's a Bridge in, wossname, Emerald City. Sure, I'm currently wanted for… for… something… but I having no way to go home is a bit scarier. Seems like I've got a goal! And, of course, I know how to get there!

She smiled and began humming a familiar showtune. Looking around, she saw a stout branch that would make a good walking stick. She grabbed it, turned, and pulled. It came loose with a satisfying snap.

"Hey!" came a voice. It was deep and grinding, and didn't seem to be entirely human.

She stared at the tree. "Was this yours? Um… sorry?" *How do you apologize for ripping off someone's limb?*

The voice, though, was behind her, not in front of her. "No, it's mine! That's my tree!"

She spun. There was another tree there, this one with an axe. Bobbi held the broken branch up defensively, realizing that it would do little more than slow down the rather large, extremely shiny, blade the newcomer held in its… branches. "Look, I'm sorry… I didn't know this was a… private… tree…"

"Damn meatbags! I'm getting sick of this! How'd you like it if I went around ripping legs off your cows, huh?"

"Hm. Do they have chainsaws here?"

The tree looked puzzled. Bobbi found the way its bark and leaves rearranged themselves into expressions to be fascinating. It didn't look either intimidated *or* angry, which were the two reactions she'd been hoping for and fearing, in that order.

"The what now?"

Bobbi sighed. Threats lost a lot of their impact when you had to explain them. "Chainsaw! It's a machine… with a saw… on… um… a chain… and it goes around very fast!" She paused for what she hoped was impact. "It's for chopping wood." She tensed, preparing to run. *I have to be able to outrun a tree*, she thought. *I mean, Tolkien said they were all slow. On the other hand, this isn't Middle Earth. This is like one of those Enterprise/Star Destroyer things… can one of these things outrun an Ent? Hmmm…* She then noticed it was neither chasing her nor quailing in fear at the thought of the weapon she clearly didn't have, but talking.

"…knew this was going to happen. It's fine if one comes along once a generation or so, but then Glinda made that deal and now we've got them crawling all over the place, and it's not like we can *do* anything to them 'cause of the 'negative economic impacts.' Blast it!"

Bobbi looked at him. "Um… what?"

The tree fixed her with an expression of utter hatred and malice. The way he had reacted to her tearing apart one of his crop was nothing compared to this. She suddenly felt a twinge of genuine fear. It had managed to move close to her, and it had a lot of branches, all tipped with a dozen waving fingers of dry, hard-edged wood. She quickly scanned the region, looking for a route that she could pass through that the tree could not.

It leaned in closer. She planned to bop it on the nose once it got in range, then flee. It spoke a word, a word of fervent loathing across all the known realities.

"Tourist."

Then it pulled back. "I'll be filing a requisition for compensation, damn straight. Meanwhile, this is private property. Get off of it."

She breathed out, slowly. "Oh… kay. Glad to. Really. Um… you have a lot of tourists here?"

"No, but one is two too many."

"Fine. Just… um… point me to the road?"

"*That* road is pretty far from here. Nearest road… head west a few miles. Enjoy the walk."

Stupid trees, she thought. First, the one which had said 'Head west.' Which the hell way was west? She hadn't thought about it at the time, but after she'd gone a bit in the direction he had pointed and then had to detour, she instinctively tried to get a GPS signal to figure out which way 'west' was… and, of course, couldn't. This was, naturally, the fault of the tree.

Second, there were all the (currently immobile) trees in front of her. And behind her. And to her sides. She'd been in uncounted forest zones in uncounted games, but they all made it relatively easy to go through, unless you weren't supposed to go at all, and that was usually made clear. You either *could* move or you *couldn't*, none of this 'move very slowly and get stuck and have to backtrack and which the hell way is west, anyway,' nonsense!

Something was stumbling through the woods, though. Something loud, clumsy, and prone to profanity. It sounded familiar.

"Matt?"

"Bobbi?" There was a sudden increase in stumbling and it got louder as it came towards her. Matt pushed his way into the smallish open spot.

She smiled. "Finally made it, huh?"

"Yes. Um... you alright?"

"Fine. So, what kind of exciting adventure did you have? I argued with a tree."

"A tree? Huh. I guess that beats a squirrel."

She nodded and tried to look wise. "Yes, yes it does." She found a convenient rock and sat down, doing her best to look as if she was entirely in control and carrying out her flawless plan. "Looks like you ended up mostly where I thought you would." She ignored his doubt-filled sneer.

"Well, tell me what happened to you."

Matt decided it was easier to just go along. "Well, first, I nearly threw up. After that..."

She laughed. "Threw up? Was the transit really rough? You *did* close your eyes, right?"

"No... I'd read you were supposed to, but since there were bullets flying, I really wasn't thinking about that 'Top 10 Trips For the First Time Traveler' articles."

"First time...?"

"For Bridging. Not for anything else. In case you were wondering."

Bobbi looked at him in stunned surprise. "You mean... you've never been off Earth before?"

Matt flushed. "Uh... no. Anyway, *after* that, I had an amusing conversation with a squirrel."

"I got a tree."

"Well, I guess we're not in..."

Bobbi glared at him. "Don't. So, did the squirrel tell you where to go?"

"Yes, but I seem to be a bit lost. How about you?"

"The tree told me where to go, but it could have done a better job. So... where to now? You're the trained sleuth."

"I mostly track things down from the US Copyright Registry web site. Still... that way. Smoke. Some kind of village, maybe? Perhaps our dead munchkin came from there?"

"And we're off. Wait a second." She looked around the small clearing, comprehension exploding onto her face. There was no way to return. Karen must have instantly shut the Bridge off to keep the cops from following them... but she was likely arrested now. The cops wouldn't have the codes... which meant...

"Matt? How are we supposed to get back?"

"I... um... shit. Huh. Well, there is the portal at Emerald City. I guess we make for there once we've found whatever we're looking for."

"Do you have any idea how to get there from wherever it is we are?"

Matt failed to not grin. "We could foll..." He saw her face. "We could ask directions. In the meanwhile... we need to investigate. Figure out what's going on."

Matt tried to take it all in. Meeting Bobbi had somewhat relaxed him. At least that was one less thing to stress over. He tried to focus on the reality of it all. He was on another world, a world fabled in... fables. He inhaled deeply. The air was cool and pleasant, with a strong scent of pine and flowers, combining to form an oddly alien, but still pleasant, scent. The sky was a brilliant blue, a bit too blue, Matt thought, and the clouds were too perfectly fluffy. It was all like walking through a storybook... which, he realized, he was.

And here I am, chasing a murder plot. It's one step away from arresting the Three Little Pigs for violations of the Endangered Species Act.

And then came the rush of running feet and the sound of bullets.

Matt pulled Bobbi back into the forest, towards the dense eastern trees – the woods thinned out considerably to the west. Someone was running, making good time, until he hit the point at which the forest thickened. There was a grunt and a stream of profanity, then the sounds of frantic struggle. A man pushed into the small clearing, panting. He was the same size as the man in Frank's apartment, horribly thin, dressed in grey clothing, which was badly torn from his frantic journey through the woods.

Matt stared through the branches, quiet, trying to assess the situation. Then it changed.

He was being followed by three winged monkeys toting machineguns.

One had a megaphone.

"Prisoner W9854! Prisoner W9854! Surrender now! You cannot escape from Royal Justice!" The beast's voice was high pitched and squeaky, and it would have been hilarious if the gun it was carefully aiming into the woods was not so palpably real and lethal looking. It was dressed in a strangely ornate uniform, yet one which was also severe and harsh – as if someone had tried to cross a band leader's uniform with that of an SS officer. Two other monkeys, wearing similar but somewhat less flashy outfits, flanked him. As the first one, which Matt was mentally calling 'Commandant Chimp' continued to speak, those two fluttered silently onwards, guns drawn.

"Your sentence is for 5 more years, Prisoner! This escape attempt will add 2 more years. Continued resistance will lead to your death!"

There was no reply, just a sudden rush of noise as the escaping man tried to bolt through the woods, only to be stymied by the dense tangle of branches. He clawed at them desperately, then turned and started to speak. He never got a word out. There was a rattle of gunfire followed by a sad, wet, thud. Commandant Chimp flew over to the source, and Matt could hear him cursing at his two aides. Matt felt Bobbi stirring besides him. He grabbed her and held her still, not sure what she was planning but knowing it wasn't going to be good. The Commandant kept yelling.

"Trigger-happy idiots! We could have grabbed him!"

"Lieutenant Nokkon, he—"

"Never mind! We will report your failure to the Commander."

One gestured down at the body. "What about…?"

"I am not going to touch that thing. Do you think you can carry it and fly?"

"No, Sir, I was just—"

"We will dispatch some of the prisoners to clean it up. If he had any friends make them do it. Let the word spread. Since you seem to care, you'll be overseeing it. Try to make sure *they* don't try to escape, either. This could end up going on for a while." He laughed, then, seemingly at the thought of an endless series of prisoners sent to retrieve the corpses of friends in the prior batch. "We need enough of them alive to meet quota, at any rate. Now come on! Punishment for your ineptitude won't get any less the longer you delay. Move! Move!"

The three flew off, the lower-ranked two flapping somewhat dispiritedly.

Matt and Bobbi waited until they were well gone. Then Bobbi crawled out from behind the branches and began to walk towards the small grove where the brief explosion of gunfire had taken place.

Matt reached out to stop her and found himself partially tangled. He began to pry himself loose while talking. "Wait… you probably don't want to…"

Bobbi paused, considered, and then moved forward. She pushed into the grove.

Photographs aren't the same, she thought. The mangled body below her was horribly real. The solidity of it, the blood, the viscera… and the smell. She was trying not to vomit. Matt was, she felt, already teetering too close to patronizing for her tastes, and she didn't want to give him more ammunition. Matt had escaped from the entangling branches and had reached her side. He didn't say anything; he just looked down at the body, his face set and expressionless.

Then he knelt and began to rummage through the bloody corpse.

Bobbi stepped back. "What are you doing?"

He paused in his search to look back to her. "As you've often reminded me, this is my job. I'm looking for clues. Information. Anything we didn't know before."

"We already know what killed him! Monkeys with machineguns!"

Neither of them smiled.

"I'm more looking for *why*. Obviously, he's an escaped prisoner… and look. He's as emaciated as the one in Frank's apartment. I'm thinking justice in Oz leaves something to be desired."

"Huh. That kind of makes sense. That was Frank's big thing, I mean, besides stealing TV shows and screwing anything he could talk into bed…” She paused. “Extra-dimensional rights. He was always going on about this or that cause. He got a lot of flak from people since he never seemed to care about the problems back on Prime… he only cared if the people who were being whipped had blue skin or fur. Hmm.”

Matt had pulled something from inside the prisoner’s outer shirt. Bobbi raised an eyebrow. “Hey, what’s that?”

Matt looked at it. It was a piece of laminated paper, slightly smaller than an index card. It was also coated with blood. “Probably some kind of identification.”

“It looks like… well, like plastic.”

“Yeah. Why is that odd?” Matt stood up and looked for something to wipe off the blood on the card, finally settling, with some reluctance, on the few clean parts of the prisoner’s own jacket. He began to study the card.

“Well… they didn’t have plastic in Oz… did they?”

“No… but it’s been a hundred years or so since the books were written. It’s a hundred years later here, too, give or take a bit. Oz always had some weird tech and the occasional visitor from their version of Earth… it makes sense they’d have advanced.”

Bobbi tried to digest this, tried to imagine an industrialized Oz, with little munchkin McDonalds, the Yellow Brick Road converted to an eight-lane superhighway, and the Emerald City engulfed in fog and surrounded by suburban sprawl. She tried to imagine it, and failed. “You’re kidding me.”

“No, not really. I don’t know what’s really happening here, what kind of society they have… but it really is about a century beyond whatever might have inspired Baum. I’m sure all that information is on file on the Infiniwiki or even the Hitchhiker’s Guide To Reality, but I didn’t really do a lot of research before meeting you. I wasn’t planning on coming here, remember. I’m kind of surprised you don’t know. Isn’t this whole ‘wonder and imagination’ thing supposed to be your specialty?”

“No, my specialty is data conversion. My *hobby* is science fiction. And Oz? Sorry, Oz is something your grandparents think is cool ’cause they remember the movie from analog television. Yeah, there are a few real fanatics who have all the first editions of the old books and stuff, but it’s not really mainstream.”

“Mainstream for nerds. Right. Sorry, I sometimes forget how cliquish you people can be about like the *wrong kind* of make-believe.” He looked down at the body. “Even when it’s real. Now, please, let me look at this."

He studied the card. "His name was Krongo, he was 28, he was sentenced for tax evasion, and there's a bunch of coded stuff I don't understand." He stopped to think. "I'm thinking we don't want to go to that prison. Call it a hunch, but I doubt they're going to be happy with foreigners poking around out here, and we're a bit too tall to pass for munchkins."

"Aren't there normal sized people in Oz? I mean, Glinda, the witch, those people in Emerald city... or maybe that was just the movie..."

"Um... damn. I can't remember who was supposed to be human sized and who wasn't. I know the movie was different from the book and that the reality is different from both. But let's face it: we can't even bluff well unless we know more than we do. We need to find someplace safe."

Bobbi pondered a second. "There ought to be a town here. If there's a prison, it's probably near a town. And the tree mentioned tourists. Tourists have to... tour... somewhere."

"The squirrel also said there was some kind of town near here... though he didn't say how near. Downhill, follow the magic invisible river..."

"There's an invisible river? Cool! What does it look like?"

Matt glowered at her. "It's invisible because I can't find it. Let me think. The monkeys came from over that way... and it looks like they flew back in a straight line. So if we walk a bit north... we ought to skirt the prison and maybe hit a road. After that, all we can do is hope the town likes tourists."

"The tree didn't. We should have brought a house. You know -- to drop on any local witches. I heard that wins 'em over."

Matt managed to laugh.

Few books, Bobbi thought, mentioned just how quickly your feet hurt when you walk long distances. Damn few games ever do either. She thought, for a moment, how she blithely steered assorted digital avatars across hundreds of miles of virtual terrain with never a thought for the condition of their toes. Barely three hours of slogging along a badly cobbled road and I am ready to gnaw my feet off at the ankles.

Of course, if I'd known I was going on An Adventure, I would have packed better shoes. Ow

She glanced over at Matt, who was managing to maintain a brisk and seemingly pain-free pace. It would not be fair to say that she hated him at that moment, but whatever positive feelings their shared experiences might have been building in her were well and truly suppressed.

Still, other than his annoying habit of not being in pain, she had to admit he was not entirely a bad sort… for a fascist whose job was to hunt down people who weren't really hurting anyone. If that word even had any meaning anymore. *I mean, hell, once you've seen flying chimps gun a munchkin down in cold blood, the bar for who gets called a 'fascist' is raised pretty high.*

A smile formed in the back of her brain and made its way to her lips.

"Are we there yet?"

Matt paused in his steady stride. "Um…what? I…" He shook his head, apparently clearing out whatever odd thoughts may have been piling up in there. "I'm not even sure where 'there' is…"

"Joke. You know, the pesky kid in the back…"

"Oh. Right. Sorry… a little lost in thought."

Bobbi welcomed the chance to take a break from the endless plodding. She sat down on a granite outcropping. "So what are you thinking about? The incredible weirdness we're living?"

He sat down beside her, trying to find, mentally, the precise distance that would not be so close as to seem presumptuous nor so far away as to seem insulting. "Um, well, honestly, at the exact time you said that… I was trying to remember if I'd fed the fish."

"Fed. The. Fish."

"Yeah. I didn't leave the apartment today expecting to go to Oz. And we might not be back for days, if that. So I was wondering 'Did I feed the fish?' And then that got me thinking about what a stupid, horribly banal thing that is to think. And then I wondered if other people thought those sorts of stupid things when they were smack in the middle of what some people would call adventures."

"You mean, like Charles Lindbergh wondering, when he was halfway over the Atlantic, if maybe he'd left the gas on at home?"

"Yeah. Like that. Or, hell, this entire conversation. We're in *Oz*, tracking down some weird conspiracy, with no friends, no idea where we're going and no way to get home, and we're sitting by the side of the road discussing Charles Lindbergh."

"Don't worry. If they ever make this into a movie, this will be the scene where we say something really profound and deep."

"How about the scene where we see a turtle on a bicycle?"

Bobbi began to say "Huh?" then looked down the road.

It was turtle. On a bicycle. One of those ancient 'penny farthing' things, which Bobbi knew about only because an old boyfriend had made her sit through an ancient spy drama. Except that this one seemed to have a complex internal combustion engine powering it. And it was being ridden by a turtle, one which seemed to be wearing complex prosthetics. It lacked prehensile fingers or the kind of legs needed to ride a bike properly, so it compensated with strap-on metallic devices. Matt wasn't entirely sure how the turtle manipulated his metal 'hands,' but it didn't seem to involve implants or surgery. Technomagic? It probably didn't matter.

Matt, for want of anything better to do, waved. The turtle looked up – Matt then saw it had a monocle – and adjusted the bike's speed. As it got closer, Matt saw that the otherwise wholly reptilian turtle sported a short white beard.

The turtle just looked down at them quizzically. The seat of the bike was some six feet off the ground, and the turtle was about four feet tall, so it had a considerable height advantage. The engine wheezed and popped as it idled.

Matt looked up at it. "Hello! Um... my name's Matt Anders, and this is Bobbi, uh, Sinderman. We're... looking for the nearest town?"

The turtle raised an eyebrow. *Turtles have eyebrows?* Thought Matt. "Well, well, well. There's a prequestionment. Nearest town's roundly twenty miles down the road."

Bobbi almost collapsed in despair. "Twenty *miles*? That's it?"

"For the nearest town, indeed!"

Matt nodded. "Where's the nearest settlement, then?"

The turtle smiled. "Oh, you're cleverish! That would be the village of Dankil. Nearbout 2 miles westouthwards." He pointed helpfully. Now that it was pointed out, Matt could see a few thin wisps of smoke from that direction.

"Many thanks, Mister, um..."

"Hephaesteus Z. Chelonian. But mostall folks just name me Bill."

Matt contemplated, for an instant, asking how one got 'Bill' from 'Hephaesteus Z. Chelonian,' but wisely decided against it. He thanked the turtle again, then began heading in the direction of

Dankil.

“We just had a conversation with a turtle on a gas powered antique bicycle.”

“Yes.”

“Just making sure that if I’m going mad, I’m doing it in company.”

It took another hour of walking to get down the road. Traffic was very light, and consisted mostly of automobiles and trucks, all somewhat oddly shaped but not spectacularly so. About a mile from town, they began to see a lot more signs of habitation – there were clearly visible farmhouses cropping up, and fields came to within a few feet of the roads, circled with high fences and barbed wire. Probably, there were scarecrows, but neither Matt nor Bobbi wanted to try finding any for a chat.

The village of Dankil was blue. Very, very, blue. Matt was unaware there were quite so many shades of blue – sky blue, azure, cerulean, robin’s egg, and a host of others. Someone who worked at a paint company could spend their whole life here and never name every shade. The people wore blue, as well, occasionally dressed up with purple or teal, but mostly blue. Blue flowers lined the streets, and bluebirds and blue jays sang in the trees.

Most of the people were short, about the size of an eight year old, but shaped in the same proportions as Prime humans. A few were taller by a foot or so, and a handful were about the same height as Bobbi and Matt. A fair number of the locals, perhaps one in ten, were clearly not human at all. They saw what appeared to be a man about to be attacked by an angry goat wearing pinstriped pants. Alarmingly, this altercation was being ignored by passersby, until they got close enough to hear the conversation, which indicated that the goat had not received the correct sandwich or toppings on his order, and the man trying to apologize while hinting, not too subtly, that the goat’s accent and pronunciation did not lend itself to easy understanding.

“Dolittles,” Matt mumbled under his breath.

Bobbi shot a sideways glance at him.

“What?”

“Sorry. Not polite. It’s a term used… a term *some people* use around the office. Non-humanoid sentient animals capable of speech.”

“Frank would have called that hate speech.”

“Sounds like Frank took a lot of things way too seriously. It’s…

shorthand. It's a way of communicating a complex concept in a few quick syllables. If someone tells you that your next assignment has a lot of Dolittles, you know what to expect. That's all."

"And it serves to reinforce insider/outsider identification, helping to promote an isolated and out-of-touch culture that dehumanizes the very people it is supposed to serve. Standard law enforcement." She smiled smugly.

"And what do you call all the various jargon, obfuscation, and so on you hacker types use?"

"That's not remotely the same thing."

"Why not?"

Something caught Bobbi's eye. "Hey, check that out. Looks like the main shopping drag. Let's see what we can find."

Dankil was not quite the Levittown Bobbi had feared, but neither did it match her mental image of what Oz should be. They walked through a downtown area of small shops and plazas, and the average level of technology seemed to be close to what Bobbi dimly remembered the 1950s were supposed to be like. Mechanical cash registers, oddly shaped cars with smoke-belching engines, and neon signs were all plainly visible. Sharp edges and hard angles were rare; most buildings adopted a roundish style of construction. Architecture by Dr. Seuss, with an assist in the color scheme by Pablo Picasso, thought Matt. Buildings and fixtures seemed to be at a wide range of scales, so that Munchkins of all sizes could use them easily. Stares and whispers, but little evident hostility, followed them.

Finally, a man in a uniform came over to them. The old-fashioned cut of the outfit, the plethora of awards and medallions, and the utter seriousness with which the four-foot high man conducted himself would have been almost comical, except for the heavy gun in his belt. He looked Matt and Bobbi up and down and then spoke.

"We don't see many dressed like you around here. You mind telling me what you've come for?"

Matt and Bobbi glanced at each other. They had, Matt realized, worked out no cover story at all. Improvisation was called for.

Bobbi blurted out "Were tourists!"

"Yes: tourists. We're… uh… tourists. Looking to see the sights of… Munchkinland." Please, please, thought Matt. Let that be the right name. Please let 'Munchkin' not turn out to be the local equivalent of the n-word…

It seems whatever gods ruled Oz were kind. The policeman nodded. "Tourists, huh?"

"Right! Here to help the local economy!" Bobbi good-naturedly added in.

"From Kansas, then?" the policeman continued.

Matt felt a small light go on. Of course. Whoever was running the Bridge had probably just used the local knowledge of an other world called 'Kansas' to smooth over any complex explanations. The government either bought the lie, or was in on the cover-up. Ah, either ignorant or corrupt. Some things cross all universe. "Yes. From Kansas."

"Huh. We don't get many of you folks down here – though we've been told to expect you." He pondered a moment, then produced a broad, if not entirely sincere, smile. "Well, welcome to Dankil! Hope you enjoy your stay!" He wandered off, waving grandly. The rest of the locals took this as a sign and immediately swarmed the two of them, many offering assorted goods for sale. Oz custom… or maybe just local practice… seemed to encourage a lot of wandering vendors and street-side storefronts. Food, toys, and items imprinted with the name of the town were all enthusiastically put forward.

Somewhere in the back of Matt's mind was the thought that Oz was supposed to be free from the scourges of capitalism, but if that had been true in the distant past or was just a fancy added by its chief chronicler, it certainly wasn't the case now. Bobbi looked at the vendors and expressed some interest in a sandwich. She reached into her pocket and produced a small plastic card. The vendor, a young woman about three feet tall, wearing an assortment of mostly-blue clothing highlighted with ribbons of green, took it, flipped it over, and frowned, handing it back.

"What's this?"

Bobbi shook her head at her own foolishness. "Sorry, sorry, of course you'll want cash…" She produced some, to be met with another rejection.

"We don't use Kansas money here. Last time a tourist came through, he had proper money."

"Um, where do I…" Matt grabbed her arm and pointed down the street.

"Bank."

Bobbi apologized to the woman. "This is why they don't like tourists, you know," Matt added. "Always assuming… aren't you supposed to be a seasoned veteran of a hundred strange and alien worlds?"

"Sorry, just a bit… overwhelmed. There's places where the whole Bridge thing is hush-hush, and there's place where it's open, but I've never been anywhere where they've got a cover story for it. That damn tree didn't really give me a lot to work with."

"We have the one edge that we're expected to be ignorant bumpkins. Let's hope that's enough to cover any more goofs."

"So, great, what do we do for money, then?"

Matt patted his pocket and then pulled out a small handful of bills. "I grabbed these when we left Brian's place… I was hoping to save them as evidence, but we have to eat." He rifled through the bills. "Not much here… and I have no idea of the exchange rate. We'll have to hope for the best. "

Fortunately, exchanging Brian's currency for the local coinage – all coins of different shapes and sizes, a vastly chaotic arrays with a nonsensical conversion system – was easy enough, though Matt was fairly sure the sly smirk on the part of the moneychanger indicated that he was a rube who had just been rooked. The pair took their newly acquired coins tried to find a place to settle down and sort out what to do next. A small park was located across from the bank. They got a number of stares, but few people wanted to bother them directly, and they were politely ignored while being kept under close observation.

They ended up sitting on a rounded blue bench in front of a stone table set with a turquoise mosaic. Even the grass, Matt noted, was a greenish teal.

Bobbi was trying to sort her coins. Paper money had never made it to Oz, it seemed. Perhaps the Cowardly Lion had retained the gold standard after all. "Great, so it's three of these to seven of those… how many sickels to a knut?"

"No, I think those are called…"

"I know what they're called. It was a joke. You haven't read those books?"

"Huh? Oh… yeah. Now I remember. Hated the ending."

"So did everyone. I know people who've spent way too much of their lives trying to get there, convinced it's out there somewhere."

Matt pondered. "That would be a nightmare. There's practically nothing they could bring back from there that wouldn't be a Class-B felony under the Revised Bono Act. It would—" He saw the expression on Bobbi's face and quickly changed the subject. "Anyway, I've been thinking about our next step. It's possible our dead munchkin came from here, or someone here might have known him. We should ask around, even check with the cops."

"The cops. The same people who, I'm guessing, send people to the chimp farm to get gunned down?"

"Or not. I'm playing a hunch. Something tells me there's a disconnect between that prison and this place."

"If your hunch is wrong?"

"We end up making license plates for the motorcycles of bearded turtles."

"Great. Can we get something to eat first? I'm starving, and if I'm going to end up in a prison camp, I want it to be on a full stomach."

Finding a restaurant was easy. There was even human scale seating, though this just made them stand out more. Matt kept glancing around nervously.

"What now?" Bobbi said.

"Just... well, I do undercover work. I like to blend in. There is nothing remotely subtle about this. Half the town knows we're here, and it's starting to get to me. If anyone's looking for us..."

Bobbi shrugged. "We order, we eat, we move on. I mean, I have a feeling the locals won't take kindly to us prowling in their back alleys. Hm. They have hamburger here."

"So?"

"Well, first, since there's probably no place called 'Hamburg' in Oz, it's kind of weird on the face of it. Second... um... talking animals? I'm not sure I want to eat food that used to have a name. "

Matt pondered this. "I'm going to *guess* that only the quiet ones get turned into food... there seems to be a caste system... of sorts. "

"I dunno... given what we've seen of the legal system so far... kick over one lantern, and, POW! You're the blue plate special."

A waitress came by, smiling with the same fixed, weary smile of waitresses throughout all known realities. Bobbi ordered a salad; Matt reluctantly picked a cheese sandwich. As the food was delivered, Bobbi's mouth twisted into a mischievous smile.

"Cheese... milk... I mean, even that's kind of like rape... think about it..." She smugly took a bit of her salad.

Matt glowered over his sandwich, then put it down. He drummed his fingers for a second, waiting. Then he looked back at her. "So, you ran into a talking tree, didn't you? Wonder how far *that* trope extends... I wonder if there's some baby lettuce out there, crying for its daddy..."

Bobbi looked down at her salad. Then she glanced around at the half-full diner, with about a dozen short, mostly happy seeming people chowing down on various dishes.

"Okay, either we're surrounded by cuddly cannibals, or, somehow, they've worked it out. Truce so we can eat?"

"Truce."

They were about half done when a group of soldiers arrived. They were instantly noticeable, as they were about twice the prevailing height – fully the same size as Matt and Bobbi, give or take a few inches. All three wore ornate red uniforms with gold trim, similar to those seen on the monkeys. Matt and Bobbi tensed. Matt shifted slightly, evaluating the situation. The three were thin, but looked to be in good health. Maybe he could take one by surprise... but there was no way to beat all three. They carried large, very visible guns at their belts, and Matt doubted they'd hesitate to open fire. One of them, the leader to judge from the excess gold trim on his outfit, talked briefly to a waiter, who pointed directly to Bobbi and Matt. The three began to move forward.

Matt saw Bobbi's fingers curling around the knife. He glanced at her.

"That's a butter knife, you know."

She dropped it and waited as the three men approached, then veered past them to sit at an adjacent booth, filling up the "human size" seats nicely. The two relaxed and tried not to keep glancing up at the seated men.

"Well, that was almost stupid," Bobbi finally said. Matt just nodded.

They continued to eat, conversation muted so as not to accidentally say anything which might call attention to themselves. Matt focused, instead, on the conversation. The bulk of it was mundane... this one was getting grief from his wife about starting a family, the other was annoyed at some kind of gambling loss... then one (whom Matt had mentally named 'Stupid Moustache') said something that set up mental alarm bells.

"...and we've got more of those Kansas men showing up every day now."

A second, the one Matt figured was the leader – "Sergeant Shiny," due to his excess of gold trim – replied, "Yeah. Sometimes I wonder who's really running the show up there."

The third one, somewhat unfairly given the mental tag of

'Tubby' due to a slight paunch as compared to his comrades, chimed in. "Doesn't bother me. We're drawing good bonuses. My brother's back at Emerald, he doesn't take home half what I—"

"Yeah, well, no one's complaining about *that* part!" said Moustache. "But they're such... weaselly bastards. Bossy. And it's sick how Nimko fawns over them."

"Nimko fawns over whomever Grobbin says to. He's Grobbin's little pet." Tubby interjected.

"Oh, like you ever stood up to Grobbin!"

"To his face – I mean, if you can call that a face? No! But Nimko's a suck-up even when no one's looking."

"It's a monkey thing, I think," added the Sergeant.

"Feh." Matt wasn't sure which of the other two made that comment. "Anyway, I'm done here. We've got some hours, might as well make use of them, right? I know a guy who knows some girls..."

The conversation then turned to certain issues of anatomy and size differential and whether or not the girls in question would notice. Matt continued to nibble slowly at his sandwich until they were gone.

"That could be useful," he said finally.

Bobbi squinted at him. "What, human women aren't doing it for you? We're going to find a munchkin pimp?"

"Not that part. The part where they're used to 'Kansas men' coming and ordering them around."

She seemed excited and leaned in. "You've got a plan?"

"Not yet. Sort of a plan of a plan. Let's see what we can learn from the cops."

The police station was a chaotic jumble of scales and species. A horse, full sized, with a captain's insignia on a sash around his neck, was dispensing orders to three munchkins in uniforms vaguely resembling those of English Bobbies from the turn of the prior century. A bored looking woman in a uniform seemingly composed of gold lame and glitter idly waved a wand over piles of paperwork, which dutifully sorted itself as she stifled a yawn and glanced at the clock. A complex automaton of some sort was standing partially disassembled against a wall, while a mechanic poked at it was what could only be described as a steam-powered wrench. Near the door, a dented bucket sat precariously balanced atop a pile of brooms.

Matt and Bobbi looked around, confused, when the pile of brooms animated itself and walked towards them. The bucket head turned, revealing eyes that were expressive and clearly painted on. It spoke, the voice issuing from the 'head,' but no mouth was visible.

"Sergeant Whisk, on duty today. Can I help you with something?"

My sanity, thought Matt, but tried to soldier on.

"Uh... I guess so... um..." He fumbled with the photographs for a second, then found the clearest one he could. "Do you, ah, know this person?"

Surprisingly agile hands of straw gently took the picture from Matt, the hundreds of small strands moving with grace and certainty. The painted, yet living, eyes, narrowed, and then, somehow, the strange and alien face managed to take on a look of very real sadness.

"Loko."

Bobbi blinked. "He was crazy? Or *we're* crazy?" Certainly, she'd been thinking it, but to have it confirmed by what had to be a delusion...

The bucket-head blinked in confusion of its own. "Hm? No, this is Loko. Lokorian Balgorad, to be formal, but we all knew him as just Loko. He had a small shop a block or two from here. Sold shoes. He was arrested for unlicensed wizardry, oh, about six months ago... About two months ago, his wife tried to visit him, and was told he'd 'escaped.'" Sergeant Whisk snorted, an amazing feat give the lack of any nose, or, it seemed any internal structure to the bucket. "No one just 'escapes' from that place."

Matt took back the picture. "Well, *he* did. Somehow. But he still managed to get himself killed."

The painted eyes took on a more serious tone. "And you are who, precisely, sir? And you are doing what with these iconographs?"

Time to up the ante, Matt thought. "I'm in the same line of work you are, Sergeant. I'm a lawman. Someone killed this, ah, Loko, and it happened on my, uh, beat, and I'm here to solve the crime."

Whisk nodded, causing the handle of the bucket to clang oddly. "Not with Her Majesty's forces though, are you, sir? No, you have the sound of tourists. From Kansas, yes? Loko made it all the way there, then? Only to die. Shame, shame."

Might as well keep to the same lie. It made things less confusing. "Yeah, we're from Kansas. We've been trying to figure out what happened to Loko." *And now we go all in.* "We, uh… we're trying to do this *without* any royal involvement." He nodded in what he hoped was a knowing fashion, and was rewarded with a warm look.

"Know what you mean, sir, I certainly do." Then he stopped and considered something. "Still, it's a bit odd, isn't it. I mean what with the Kansas men running the prison and all." Something dark passed over the metal-and-paint visage. "You wouldn't be loyalty officers, would you now? Because that would be a mean trick to play…"

Matt was suddenly aware that the seemingly random and milling crowd of police had fallen into an entirely non-random circle around them and, while he wasn't sure what weapons they handed out to cops in Munchkinland, the odds were good that they could kill lions, tigers, and overly-nosy FBI agents mistaken for the Secret Police.

"No, no! We're not, Sergeant. We're trying to find out what's going on here. Our laws – Kansas laws – don't allow us to make those kind of deals. I think… I think some of our people might be doing something very illegal up there."

Whisk glared at them, then gave a sidelong glance at woman in the gold lame, who was now holding a small glass sphere in which a red vapor swirled. She nodded sharply.

Whisk's expression softened instantly, and the circle fell back into its constituent chaotic components. "Well, good enough for me, then." A broomstick arm gestured for the two to follow. They did.

The room was blue, of course, but the large table in the middle was made of solid oak, ornately carved. The chairs surrounding it resembled mid-'50s office chairs as designed by Dr. Seuss, but they were comfortable enough. A pitcher of ice water, half-melted, sat in the center of the table, as did four bluish glasses. Bobbi and Matt sat down. Sergeant Whisk did not – suddenly, Matt realized, he didn't bend that way.

Does he get tired? Does he have blood? Do his feet… er… bristles hurt after a long day of policing? So many questions, and it's probably rude to ask them. Even more, it's irrelevant. I've got a murder to solve, a case actually worth *solving for the first time in my career, and I'm going to solve it – even if it means talking to a broom.*

The broom in question suddenly slapped his head, causing a metallic ringing sound. "You'd think my head was filled with straw, not just my hands! I need to get the files! One moment, please!" He then scuttered away.

Once he left, Bobbi began waving her cell phone in a slow arc around the room. "This is great! I've been getting shots of the whole town! No one would believe me if I didn't have some kind of proof!" For the moment, the ransacking of her apartment – and the fact she was a wanted fugitive – seemed to have been put on the back burner.

"It might all be faked. Cooked up in Photoshop or even a modeling program."

Bobbi shook her head. "Not with this baby. Everything it does is watermarked and tagged with a hardware based encryption key. It's about impossible to fake." She flipped it over and showed him the seal on the back. "Courtroom certified digital security. Hmm. Surprised you don't have one."

"I'm surprised you *do*. That's a pretty expensive option."

"The people I work for can be occasionally generous."

"Yes but… why? Were you planning on being a photojournalist or a PI?"

She laughed. "Because it's *cool*. Because it's *new*. Because it's something *not everyone else has*. Including, for example, people who actually *do* work in law enforcement." She smirked at him with mock malice.

Sergeant Whisk returned, carrying a bundle of documents. The "files" were a mélange of mundane paperwork, ornate and ribbon-bedecked scrolls, and two thin pieces of wood riddled with holes. Whisk seemed to notice Bobbi turning one over in her hand with rapt interest.

"Oh, that's a…"

"Tiktok programming card? I've heard of them, I've just never seen one before…" She turned to Matt. "Notice how the holes are different sizes? It's not just a simple binary system; they use the size and even the angle of the hole to encode a great deal of info…" She then saw the familiar glaze pass over his eyes, the glaze she often encountered when dealing with those to whom technology was just a means to an end, and not an end in itself. She sighed and placed the small board on the desk.

"So what do we have here, anyway?" Matt began to filter

through the documents. There was a form indicating Loko's commitment... there was a set of newspaper clippings detailing the construction of Her Majesty's Royal Prison of Munchkinland... a form declaring Loko a 'fugitive from justice'... and assorted other paraphernalia. "I'm sorry, Sergeant, but I can't make much sense of these dates... we, ah, use a different calendar back in Kansas. Can you tell me about how long ago Loko, um, escaped?"

"A month ago, it was."

Matt tried to do some math. The raid on Frank's had been two weeks past. If time passed as the same rate, that gave Loko two weeks to somehow find a way to Prime and get picked up by Frank. Hm.

"How far is it from here to the Emerald City? If you were on foot, and starving, and a fugitive?"

Whisk gave it some thought. "A long walk, certainly. A month or more. If you hitchhiked, or stole a vehicle... a lot less."

"Is it likely Loko could have done that?"

Whisk shook his metallic head. "No. Not with the brand on him."

"Brand?"

"A mystic mark, a purple star on the forehead. It marks one as a prisoner, and no one would give aid. As for stealing... well, a desperate enough man might, I suppose, but I don't think Loko was the type. Besides, why head to the Emerald City? What more foolish place could a branded man go to?"

Bobbi, who had once more picked up the program card and had begun turning it over and over in her hands, set it down on her lap. Then she grabbed the pictures from the table and flipped through them.

"Matt... look, here's a clear shot of his forehead... no star!"

Whisk just nodded. "Well, of course. No magic in Kansas. That's part of why Loko always wanted to go there. He kept on and on about it, how strange and eerie it must be."

"Hunh. Whisk..."

The Sergeant bristled, somewhat literally. "Sergeant Whisk, if you please, sir."

"Of course. Sorry. Sergeant Whisk, how often do people try to escape that prison?"

"More often than I'd like to tell. It's a hellish place, I hear, where the guilty labor long and hard to work off their offenses to Her Majesty... Work more than's fair, I'd say."

"But with the brand, they can't just vanish into the community, can they? So where do they think they're going?" Pieces began to fall into place...

"I don't know. Perhaps they run outside of Her Majesty's laws to some lost, little village somewhere... but those are far from here. Desperation can make a man do desperate things..."

"So can hope. I think there's a way into Kansas near that prison."

Whisk's eyes widened. "That could be, yes. I've heard people say the Kansas men come and go without passing by the eastern towns..."

"I think we've got it. Sergeant, you've been a great help, and I think you may have made poor Loko's death count for something. Just one thing – what's the fastest way to that prison?"

"Commit a crime against her Majesty."

For an instant, Matt was taken aback, but then he saw the glint in the painted eyes.

"From Kansas to Oz, cops love gallows humor."

"Yes, we surely do. Don't worry. I can give you directions, but I have to warn you... if you get into trouble snooping about, I can't help you. It's Royal, not County, law that holds up there."

Matt nodded. "We'll be careful. If not... we won't mention you."

"Good luck to you, then. And if you solve it, come back and visit me and the wife sometime."

For an instant, Matt tried to wrap his mind around a broom-and-bucket having conjugal relations with another broom-and-bucket... or with a flesh-and-blood woman... and then decided to put those images in a deep, dark, corner of his mind where only he and his therapist would ever see them. From the look on Bobbi's face, a similar process was going on with her... then again, her hand gestures seemed to indicate she was working out the actual details as opposed to studiously avoiding considering them.

Matt nudged her along, sensing she was about to start asking indelicate questions.

It was massive, looming, and grey – not at all the sort of place one tended to associate with Oz. Matt wasn't sure what he had expected. Gay, colorful, ribbons on the barbed wire? The crenellations of the watchtowers were a bit more ornate and pointy than those on Prime, but that didn't do much to offset the gloom. The prisoners were not singing while they worked, but shuffling listlessly.

They were a on a hill, looking down. A lone road made its way between tall cliffs, with a single exit to the prison. Small black specks fluttered here and there, purposefully – monkey patrols. The design of the prison seemed pretty standard – a large central building, some three stories tall, surrounded by a work yard with a number of farms and outbuildings. A *large* number of outbuildings. The amount of open space in the yard was very small, and the glass-enclosed structures which filled it seemed to take over every square foot. Looking closely, Matt could see that one was under construction in an area that seemingly also held a field of crops that were being torn up by the inmates.

"So now what?"

"Now… we lie. A lot."

He stood up and adjusted his suit. It was a bit worn, a bit shabby, and stained in one or two spots. He ran some fingers through his hair, trying to turn the tangled mop it had become into something that looked Severe and Official. He turned to Bobbi, intending to ask her if she had a mirror or a comb, then thought better of it. She didn't seem like the mirror and comb type. If he needed a universal data interface adapter, maybe.

"How do I look?" he finally asked.

"Like an Nerd Patrol agent who has spent the last twelve hours or so on the run across two universes."

"Just what I was hoping for. Well, let's do this thing."

They walked down the hill. They were sure to have been seen, but, presumably and hopefully, random passers-by weren't shot out of hand. Presumably. Hopefully.

It seemed that was the case – at least as long as the passersby were heading very openly and without secrecy towards the main prison gates. *Why bother pouncing on the mouse just as he's walking for the trap*? Matt thought.

They got to within about twenty feet of the gate when a clear, amplified, voice called out for them to "Halt!" and then to "State your business!"

Matt held aloft his FBI badge, hoping that this would mean something here – if everyone "in on it" was from the Bureau, they could use the badges to show the locals they were on the same team. Otherwise... he didn't want to think about it too much.

"Matt..." What if his name had already been leaked? Damn it. "Feischman. Matt Feischman." He put away the badge and ID, which now no longer matched his name. *If I'd known, I could have requisitioned psychic paper. Oh well.*

The guard, gaudily attired as they all were, the only obvious color in the area, frowned. He mumbled something to one his comrades and then gestured for Matt to come forward.

"Your business here? We weren't expecting..."

"My business here isn't with you. We've heard of problems with this place, and I'm here to straighten them out." *Bluff, bluff, bluff...* "Your name is..." Matt made a show of searching the guard's chest for identification, but he saw nothing. Maybe name badges weren't the fashion here?

The guard stammered for second, his normally rehearsed speech sent veering off track. Matt pressed the advantage. "Well, out with it! Of course, given what I've been hearing, it wouldn't surprise me that this place hires idiots who can't even remember their own names..."

"Drollvik... Senior Watchman Drollvik... I... I think you had better talk to..."

What was that name from the restaurant? Nimko? Matt leapt into the guard's speech. "I want Nimko. Can you get me to him, Drollvik?" Matt made the name sound like a curse.

Drollvik nodded. Like all professional bullies, he respected anyone more evidently in charge than he was. Still, his eyes narrowed suddenly. "Who's *she,*" he asked, pointing at Bobbi.

"No one. My assistant." As the inevitable angry fume began, Matt kicked her lightly in the shins and made a frantic, angry, gesture which he hoped, somehow, on some alternate world, was sign language for 'shut up and play along or we'll be killed by flying monkeys'.

Drollvik seemed to accept this. He reached down and pulled some curved levers on a device that looked like the illegitimate offspring of an old-style manual typewriter and a diseased pipe organ. There was a sudden burst of sound, a twisted sequence of notes, and something that Matt had assumed was a boiler used during the winter times unwrapped itself and approached them.

It was mostly cylindrical, with arms like jointed monkey wrenches and a spherical head with miniature signal lanterns for eyes. Steam poured out of it, mostly from two large smokestacks, but also from random joints and holes where it was partially rusted through. Every time it moved, it sounded like a car in a car crusher, making its way to automobile heaven.

"Nimko!" Drollvik shouted at it. "Nim! Ko!" The thing stood immobile for a second, then there was a horrible clatter, the sound of a thousand nickels tumbling in the clothes dryer of the gods, and it made a creaking, nodding, gesture. An unnoticed grate split open in its round head, revealing the fires of Baal glowing behind, and it said "FOL. LOW."

Matt and Bobbi did. Bobbi did more than follow; she was practically in love, watching its every move and gibbering under her breath. *We are walking to the guillotine,* Matt thought, *and her main concern is the elegance of the latch mechanism.*

The walk to the main door took them past considerable frenzied activity. Well, perhaps 'frenzied' was too strong a term. There were prisoners, dozens of them, performing all kind and manner of labor, but they did so with a slow languor that seemed to come more from exhaustion than from dissidence. One fell, and was booted until he somehow managed to pull himself up. When Matt and Bobbi were spotted, the guards – a mix, Matt noticed, of humans, munchkins, monkeys, and at least one badly scarred and angry looking grizzly bear – redoubled their efforts to get the prisoners to work.

They didn't seem to be engaged in random busywork. There was no one making large rocks into small rocks. Rather, there was a lot of building and clearing. They constructs looked like greenhouses, with rather ornate and complex mechanisms attached to them. With nothing else to compare them to, it seemed the machines were some kind of air pumps or filters, all done with the Ozian love of over-complication and massive amounts of pipes and gearwork. *Then again, I have no idea what the laws of physics are here. These could be bleeding edge designs, smooth and simple, the iPods of Oz.*

The creature in front of them continued its slow, purposeful, march. They passed through another set of gates, much stronger than the outermost. It seemed the outer area was considered a minimum security yard, with the inner courtyard a more secure area. Matt also noticed that the stonework here was much more worn. Older? Had the prison been expanding? Who knew?

Their guide stopped at the gate with a hiss of escaping steam. Bobbi looked over at it.

"They were supposed to be more clockwork than steam... maybe they've advanced. Or maybe this is a new model... or an old one..."

She began to reach for its back, where a control panel of sorts was visible under a layer of rust and grease. Matt tapped her on the shoulder and pointed.

A well-dressed winged chimp was standing – well, hovering – in front of them. His uniform was blue, and quite well cut. Small bangles decorated his wings. He wore tiny, wire-rimmed glasses that were engineered to fit perfectly on his face. Matt looked at him closely. The size of the brain case was the same as that of any Prime chimp… but they seemed to be fully sapient. Then again, if a goat… *or a bucket*… can be, the laws here are *really* different.

"Gentlemen…" the monkey began hesitantly. His voice was high pitched, but clear and articulate. "This is an unexpected… honor. Tell me, what can I do for you?"

"Nimko, is it?"

"Of course, we've…" Nimko peered closely at Matt's face, lifted his glasses and looked again. "No, no I suppose we haven't. Sorry. You all…" He stopped before adding 'look alike,' fumbled a bit, and then tried to recover with "…deserve my full respect and attention. But there wasn't to be a meeting for a week yet." He set the glasses back on this face. "What can I do for you," he asked again.

Keep up the bluff, Matt thought. "You can explain what kind of shithole crap operation you're running here, Nimko. Back in Kansas, we're getting pretty pissed."

Nimko flapped back a few feet. "I… I am sorry, sir, I don't understand. Last week, you said you were…"

"Last week was last week! You haven't seen me before, that's because I wasn't *needed* before. They only send me out when things aren't going right, got it? So if I'm here now, what does that tell you?"

"But… I… we met…"

"I need a baseline. I've read the reports, but I've stopped trusting the people who write them. Give me the grand tour, now, and make sure there's nothing I need to see that I don't!"

Matt hadn't known a chimp could blanche, but Nimko did.

"Of course… please, come along."

Bobbi sidled up to him and whispered. "Damn, you must have got an A+ in Fascist 101. I am impressed. Didn't think you had it in you." She pondered a moment. "Kind of repulsed that you did, actually."

"Thanks so much. Now can I pay attention?"

"Is… is something wrong?" Nimko had heard the whispering,

but hopefully not the contents.

"No. Just giving my assistant instructions. She can be a little slow. Ow!"

"Sorry, *boss*. Didn't see your shin there, where my foot was."

Nimko seemed to consider saying something, then decided, in the manner of all good toadies, that if he didn't know precisely the right thing to say, it was better to say nothing, just to nod and smile. So he did.

"Naturally. Come this way, please."

The prison tour went on for an hour, and Matt was having trouble figuring out what he was supposed to be figuring out. There was nothing that leapt out and screamed: "This is the Top Secret Key To The Whole Puzzle." Not that it wasn't interesting in that horrifically banal way such things are.

"The main cell blocks are here, of course," Nimko was going on. "We've been engaging in some creative arrangement to maximize prisoner holding while not requiring any additional housing space." He fluttered past a cell in which twelve tiny bunk had been stacked. Matt judged the cell would hold one prisoner on Prime, maybe two; more than that and the ACLU would have been reconsidering their position on the Second Amendment. "It's all in the regulations, you see, we've had excellent luck in getting permission to adjust them as you fellows have recommended. You are clever in Kansas, sir, certainly..."

Matt looked at the currently empty cell. "Yes, very well, but why is the door so large? Looks like it's designed for, well, normal folks."

If Nimko, who was of Munchkin height himself, took umbrage at the implication he was abnormal, he wisely made no sign of it. Matt realized he wasn't sure just how overbearing he was supposed to be or what they expected, but 'arrogant bully' was working so far, and there didn't seem to be any limit on how high he could turn the knob.

"Well, yes, it *was*, but as I was saying, we've been playing with the regulations... the, ah, the normal people, as you say... well, they do perhaps twice the work of the munchkins prisoners, but consume far more than twice the space or food, so..."

"Square cube law" muttered Bobbi.

"Ignore her," Matt said to Nimko. "I always do! Assistants, right?" A small bit of bonding a little 'We're all men... and monkeys... of the world here' might help. A lot of bullying, a little praise… standard technique. Fascist 101, as Bobbi put it. This time, he dodged her foot.

"So, fine, you've got the housing issue settled. What's down that way?"

Nimko seemed puzzled. "You're interested in that?"

"I'm interested in *everything*. We've had reports, Nimko, troubling reports."

"Sir, if you could just tell me what… perhaps I could help you focus and you could be done sooner, enjoying the local scenery…"

Hm. It might be interesting to add a small bit of meat to the bone of bluff. "Loko. Remember him?"

Nimko stared blankly. "No… no, I can't say I do. I am so sorry, Sir, was this someone who worked here or…"

Matt put on his best angry glare. "No, he was a prisoner here. Emphasis on *was*. He escaped. A few weeks ago."

"Well, sir, I'm sure he'll be caught eventually."

"He was."

Nimko almost hurt his face, so broad was the fake smile. "Well, then, there you go!"

"In. Kansas."

Nimko almost fell to the ground. Since the hovering seemed to be instinctual, that was impressive.

"Suh… sir?"

That had an impact. Matt pushed.

"Yes. In Kansas. I don't think I need to tell you how much *trouble* that could cause for us. And if we're having trouble…"

"Then… but… no, no, that cannot be."

Matt pulled out his own photos of the crime scene. "Look familiar to you?"

"These… these came from Kansas?"

"Yes."

"I don't… I don't see how…"

"He was here for unlicensed magic, wasn't he?"

Nimko shrugged. "Honestly, sir, I don't pay attention to who is here for what… I just oversee the guards… I doubt even the warden knows…"

The other name from the restaurant. The warden? Probably. "Grobbin. Yes, maybe we should ask him."

Oh, that did it. "No, no, that won't be necessary. I'll make sure the guards are disciplined. And the prisoners… oh yes. We can use this sir! Another round of regulations! We can get a lot more assigned to the special duty, sir, and the EC won't have any reason to get suspicious!"

Now, *that* was helpful. "*Have* they been getting suspicious?"

"No... well... not really. It's all a matter of balance, you know. We need to have 'disciplinary problems,' of course, or we don't have enough, but if we have too many, they send their own inspectors out..." He paused a moment. "Of course, the income helps. We're the cheapest prison in the system, and that keeps a lot of them quiet. We also reinvest some of the surplus in smoothing over matters..."

"You bribe the inspectors."

Nimko smiled. "Of course, sir, of course. You didn't think we were skimming, did you?"

"I am here to find out what I think, Nimko. Remember that."

"Of course, of course... Now, let us..."

A prisoner was walking by. He saw Nimko and immediately cowered back. Unfortunately, this caused him to trip over an (apparently non-sapient) bucket that had been placed on the floor. He went sprawling, his uniform catching on a bit of guardrail and tearing, the box he was carrying flying out of his hand to scatter its contents across the floor.

Nimko turned on him, his face contorted in twisted fury, the simpering expression he had worn an instant before dissolving like a witch in a thunderstorm. If he hadn't been wearing a fancy, expensive, uniform, thought Matt, he'd be producing some feces to fling. Nimko flapped towards the cowering prisoner in a tooth-baring rage, utterly oblivious. Bobbi knelt down to pick up one of the bottles.

It was a small pill bottle of orange plastic, much like those of Prime. Bobbi had adjusted to the idea of a modernish Oz. She thought that it was an amusing coincidence that the bottles were so similar, until she looked at the label.

This was *from* Prime. Or from a world virtually identical. The bar codes were the same length and pattern, and she recognized the hospital name. She'd been there once with a twisted ankle. Matt was still looking Stern and Official, as Nimko continued to screech incoherently at the prisoner. Two human guards were running up, metal truncheons in hand. She tapped Matt on the shoulder and made him look at the bottle.

He frowned, then whispered to her. "Amphetamines?"

"Yeah. From Prime, almost certainly. So what's the deal here?"

"I… I don't know. Smuggling drugs in? Maybe… maybe this is a distribution center? They buy drugs from our boys, sell them in Oz, split the profits? But… why the prisoners, then? It's not like they're helping sell the drugs or anything…"

Nimko had almost calmed down now, watching as the two guards pounded the poor man as he curled up, cowering. Matt struggled not to look away, not to interfere, to even contort his face, as best he could, into an approving smile. The man's whimpers were reduced to pathetic, wracking, sobs.

He was a bit healthier looking than the two escapees Matt had seen, though. Not exactly round and roly-poly, but not the hideous near-skeletons the others were. Different grade? Got different food?

Nimko stood over the shivering figure, then reached down and plucked out an identification card from the uniform. "Jarrik, Jarrik… you'd think that with so little time left you'd be more careful…" Nimko kicked at the torn rags of the uniform. "Destruction of government property… I'm afraid that's a Category Green offense." The chimp's muzzle twisted into a wicked, tooth-baring grin. "Assign him to Special Production."

At that, the man gained back some of the energy the beating had taken out of him. "No… no… only two months to go… sir, please, sir, I've never… my first…" Nimko shook his head and laughingly tossed a pill bottle towards Jarrik. "You shouldn't be spilling these, Jarrik, you'll be needing them…" He laughed some more, then turned to Matt and Bobbi as the screaming Jarrik was hauled off, his tiny legs beating furiously and futilely as the two guards treated him with as much effort as they'd need to handle a somewhat petulant toddler.

Matt wasn't sure where to take the bluff now. For a moment, he had thought maybe the deal was providing drugs to keep the prisoners easily controlled… but what kind of lunatic would give prisoners uppers? It was possible the drugs worked differently here… but some of it still didn't make sense. There was more. Well, might as well keep pushing on it.

He picked up one of the bottles, making sure Nimko saw him. "Is this how you handle the stuff we provide?" That was vague. Hopefully, Nimko would fill in the details.

"No, no… you saw! We punished him! We're very careful with this, very careful… It's in our interests too, you know!"

Matt nodded as if he did know, though he didn't. "Why don't you show me?"

Nimko seemed surprised. "Well, there's some observation areas... you'll need to be careful, sir, there's always a little leakage... the filters aren't as good as they could be, you know..."

Matt frowned. "Then maybe *that's* your problem. Why don't we look at the filters, then?"

Nimko seemed even more lost. "Ah... as you wish, sir."

Bobbi gave him a look of confusion, holding her hands out in a gesture of 'What are you *doing?*' He just shrugged back at her.

They were taken down. The prison evidently had quite a bit of underground to it. He noticed something else, that there was grey metal on the walls, gridwork which didn't quite form bars or squares or any other pattern. He tapped at it; it was soft and dull.

Nimko glanced at him. "Lead, of course. Antithaum. We have a lot of magicians here, keeps them in line."

"Not Krongo, and he wasn't even a magician" Matt added. Let's open another wound, see what bleeds out.

"An accident. We thought... well, normally, once they're in Special Production, there's not much they can do. Sometimes... sometimes..." His voice trailed off. "Krongo just escaped this morning. No reports have been filed. How did..."

Oh, great, I've made the chimp suspicious.

He tried to look bored and contemptuous. "Nimko, you really do run an amateur operation here. Do you think we don't have people here you don't know about? And don't go running a witch-hunt for them, either. We'll know, and we won't be happy."

Nimko's face returned to its normal fawning expression, but there was something new behind the eyes, something that glistened with dark malice. *He knows something's up, but he's not sure what or how to react. Great. Time to find some way to ease out of here...*

"Here's the main workshop. We moved most of this down here recently, we need the upper areas for the greenhouses, of course." Four guards, big burly types who strained their ornate uniforms to the breaking point, were there. They saluted sharply when Nimko approached.

"They want to see the manufacturing room. Let them in."

One nodded and produced a ring filled with oversized keys of gold and silver. There was a click, and the door opened, and the faint sound of hammering and pounding became a much louder din.

There were a few dozen people there. Mostly people. A mule was hauling metal back and forth, and the fact it had an identification card strapped to its neck indicated it was a prisoner, not a mere beast of burden. There was someone there who might have been made from rags and ribbons, and one person who was made, it seemed, entirely from porcelain, and who now looked as if he had been bashed to bits and reassembled by a clumsy child. He was doing something with gears and moving like a man crippled with arthritis… which was, Matt reasoned, likely to be how he felt.

There were only two guards in here, at least, only two human guards. There was also a massive pile of clockwork and gears, a spikier, heavier, cousin of the machine which had brought them from the gate to the door. It walked the room, its whirring head turning this way and that, watching for any sign of disorder.

Nimko gestured grandly. "There you go. Here's where we make all the machinery. We don't order anything from the outside, except parts… this is all 'occupational therapy,' you know. Everything's here… the filters for the greenhouses, and the equipment we use in post processing." Matt noticed he was fawning a lot less, all of a sudden. "Is there anything else you want to see?"

Matt scrambled for a topic, any topic. He thought that saying 'No' wouldn't work – he hadn't really seen enough to deliver any kind of report. But what to see next? He had one straw to grasp at…

"Post processing. I think that's where the trouble might be."

Nimko smiled thinly. "Of course." He turned to lead them further down. "It is this way, through the hall. We want it to be secure."

Then there was a sudden sound of running and shouting. Matt turned. There were two people there… humans… dressed much like himself. He was too far to identify them clearly, but they were both middle-aged men in suits. They were accompanied by…

It was gorilla sized, or perhaps a bit larger. The parts of it that were apish were dressed in a bright blue uniform, oddly cut and tailored, but covered with enough gold trim to outfit an entire middle school marching band. The other parts of it… about half of its body… was a strange collection of gears, pipes, venting steam, and metal plating. It glared down at them, and its metal arm swung around to point, then stuck. While Matt watched, someone, a munchkin in a guard's uniform, ran forward holding a gargantuan key, as if from some strange wind-up doll, and began cranking it. The thing moved again almost as soon as the cranking began.

Nimko spun. "I knew it! Knew something was wrong with you

two! Guards…"

Bobbi's foot swung up, aiming for his crotch. She missed as he fluttered back. He laughed, then Matt swung at him with a vicious overhand chop and pounded him into the ground. He was light, surprisingly so. Thin bones? Probably.

"Now what?" Bobbi looked at him, and at the guards, who had recovered from their momentary surprise and were moving in.

"Run!"

Bobbi looked around. She tried to use her long years of gaming experience to form a tactical assessment. Unfortunately, she realized quickly, absolutely nobody had a colored 'friend or foe' circle on their feet, there was no radar HUD, and worst of all, there'd be no respawn if things went wrong.

Still, some things could be applied.

When all else fails, cause chaos.

She ran, as Matt instructed. She ran to the spike covered guardian machine, whose spring-powered brain was evidently not entirely up to the task of dealing with capturing non-prisoners even when being directly ordered to do so. As gears and cogs slowly processed Nimko's barked orders, Bobbi ducked – barely – under a swinging metal arm and jammed the wooden board she'd "borrowed" from the police station into a well-marked input slot. She wasn't sure what, if anything, it would do, but she saw no other option for action.

The result was dramatic. Bobbi had to take a few seconds off from frantically ducking bullets to admire her handiwork.

The ponderous thing came roaring to sudden, violent, life. It raged. Huge arms of metal spun madly, smashing tables, machinery, and walls. The porcelain man backed up slowly, agony writ on his glazed face, in order to avoid a final encounter. The mule made a hawing noise, then coughed, and then began issuing well-articulated profanity. The guards diverted their attention from Bobbi and Matt and focused it on the crazed machine.

Matt dodged debris and got next to her.

"What the hell did you do?"

She shrugged. "Got me. I had no idea what that board was coded for. I was hoping mostly to jam or crash the thing, but apparently I got 'Go Psycho 1.0.' Now what?"

Matt looked around. The creature's flailing had turned the workroom to chaos, but it was starting to buckle under constant gunfire. Their reprieve would be brief. Then he saw it. One of the thing's blows had smashed open a wall, and behind it was... a passage?

He pointed to it. "Through there!"

"Do we know where it goes?"

"Out of here! What else matters?"

"Good point."

They ran for the opened tunnel, even as the mad machine's fury caused a further collapse of the room. Bobbi hoped the porcelain man survived.

The passage was dark and dank, the only light coming from the partially blocked entrance. "Where are we? Who builds prisons with secret passages?"

Matt slowly felt his way along. It was curved slightly upwards. There were things on the walls. He touched one. There was a slight grinding sound, and a pinhole opened. He peered through it, and saw the battle raging in the room. The mule kicked a monkey in the chest, sending it flying into the path of the machine, where it was struck hard. Blood and brains flew in an arcing spray; the wings fluttered madly for a second and the body dropped, still slightly twitching.

"Observation... someone liked to watch. With luck, this should take us anywhere we want to go."

"Which would be great if we had any idea where we wanted to go."

"We go up, first. Then... westish. West. We want to move as far from the main building as we can."

"If it even goes that far."

"I'm waiting for your better plan..."

"West it is!"

They moved. It looked as if there was going to be no immediate pursuit; perhaps it was assumed they were buried under the rubble which blocked the entrance. If so, they'd have only a few minutes lead before diggers found, firstly, no bodies, and second, the very obvious hole.

There was very little light, only a few dim spots of illumination where small shafts angled downwards from cracks or holes. Matt mentally added 'flashlight' to his list of things to bring with him on a regular basis. They tried to balance speed and quiet. Every so often, Matt stopped to take a look at the workings of the prison.

One room in particular interested him. There were no human, munchkin, or monkey guards, just two smaller tik-toks. The prisoners were among the most emaciated he'd seen, many trembling, and all were working at small, complex machines. Piles of red leaves were dumped in front of them, and they were feeding them in. He yawned, feeling the exhaustion of the past few hours taking its toll. Shouldn't have stopped, he thought, not even for a moment... then someone screamed, jolting him partially awake. One of the workers, a tiny, thin, man with tufts of bright orange hair sticking out at odd angles, had leapt up and begun tearing at himself, saying nothing, just screaming. Two of the others saw this and went to him, tried to hold him down, even as his hands and chest became soaked with blood from his frantic clawing. The machines moved into action. One pulled the screaming man from his two friends. Matt watched, eyelids beginning to droop, as the other machine went to bloody man and, with a final crack, silenced his screaming and stilled his motion.

"That's... just... so..." He started to slump. Bobbi caught him.

"No time... for naps. Not that I... don't understand..."

Matt struggled to hold on to consciousness. "Away... away... move up... shut hatch... away..." His thoughts began to meander, reality slipping. From somewhere, there was a click, and the feeling of motion.

Consciousness struggled to return, then came more quickly when his head slammed against concrete. Pain brought him back, and he looked up to see a slumped Bobbi.

"Sorry..." she murmured. "You were heavy..." Her voice was distant, with a faint hint of stoner giggle.

He pushed himself forward, upwards. "Come on... up some more... got to clear the area..."

They crawled forward. Another foot, then another, their heads slowly clearing.

Bobbi made it to her feet. "Wow. What hit us?"

"I think," Matt said, holding his head as he managed to stand. "I know what's going on here, mostly."

"What?" She was standing now, holding to the walls until she was sure.

"Poppies."

Bobbi's face contorted in a look of confusion for a second, then cleared itself. "You mean..."

"Yeah. That must have been some kind of processing room. No living guards. They'd be asleep, just like we almost were."

"So how do the prisoners do it? They'd..." She stopped. "The uppers."

"Right. Keep the prisoners jacked up to an amazing degree, they can do the work. Prime supplies the drugs, probably bought through connections. This prison supplies the processed poppies. Magical drugs."

Bobbi shook her head. "No, no... look, I, uh, didn't do much of that stuff myself... but, y'know, I knew people. If there was something new on the streets, I'd know. This has been going on a while."

"They're almost certainly not running the stuff to Prime. Probably doesn't even work there. But there's got to be worlds where it does work, once you set up the route... How long can you hold your breath?"

"About a minute. Why?"

"Can you get back there and grab some pictures? We might need them."

She nodded. "Pull me out if I fall, okay?"

"Sure."

Despite some wooziness, it wasn't difficult to get the shots. Bobbi managed to capture even the broken corpse, tossed in a corner until it could be picked up.

"One thing I don't get... the guy who freaked. Why kill him like that?"

Matt shrugged. "Casual cruelty? I don't know... that would cut into the profits. Maybe... maybe the constant mix of uppers and poppy fumes gets to you, makes your brain finally explode? Once it happens, you're no use, so..."

"Maybe. Back to getting out of here?"

"Yeah. We're up somewhere... there's got to be a door somewhere, an entrance..." There was a clunk. "Okay, that's the end of this part of the hall. Feel around..."

It took a few minutes. There was an increase in noise from far down the passage, and they realized the hole had been uncovered.

"Great, just... hey! Some kind of..." There was a click. A part of the door slid back. They were face to face with nightmare.

It was the figure they'd seen back in the machinery room, but now they were looking at it up close. A badly scarred simian face, torn partially in half, the other half replaced with irregular, dull grey machinery. Gears and springs could be seen churning away inside the partially open enclosure. A metal hand ending in a gripping claw swung up, even as the half-flesh, half-clockwork mouth opened in surprise. A single wing beat furiously in anger, unable to even partially lift the armored torso.

"You!" the thing – Matt realized this was Grobbin, the warden – gasped. His voice was half-squeak, half-terrible grinding sound.

Bobbi had poked her head over Matt's. "Wow: a borg chimp!"

Grobbin didn't seem to understand the comment, but simply moved to attack. His body was massively powerful, and fast, but clumsy and inflexible. Matt ducked, dropped down, spun, and brought his foot up, hoping against hope that *those* parts weren't armored.

The high-pitched squeal of pain told him they weren't. Even as Grobbin staggered back, his metal arm moved in a heavy arc, catching Matt in the side. Matt felt ribs crack. Grobbin move forward in an odd, unbalanced, gait, leering. "You have any idea what trouble you've caused? Your people, your Kansas men… they'll be happy to see you locked away here. You are going to… suf… fer…"

His metal body stopped moving. The flesh part continued to reach for Matt, who was scooting back, but a lightweight organic body designed for flight lacked the muscle to haul what looked like two or three hundred pounds of wrought iron. Bobbi walked around the now mostly inert Grobbin, holding in her hands a large key.

"Fundamental weakness of windup technology." She smirked, then dropped the key in her purse. "Let's run, before someone comes in to give him his afternoon windup. Hmm. That sounds really dirty, somehow."

"One second." Matt leapt for the desk, and grabbed a handful of random papers. "Something here… Something could be useful."

"Fine. We have to go."

"Got a plan? In case you missed it, we're in a *prison.* They're harder to get out of than get into. Sort of the *point.*"

Bobbi looked at the key, studying it. She ran her fingers along the complex grooves and notches, then looked back to Grobbin and smiled. "So I'm thinking you couldn't put a steam burner in that hunk of metal and not roast what's left of your body, so they had to go back to good old windup. I'm also betting this key is pretty special, that there aren't a lot lying around, and if anything were to happen to it… So I'm thinking we have a bargaining chip… er… key."

Grobbin blinked and muttered something. Bobbi pouted, then walked behind him. "Okay, you need a little winding to speak. But here's the deal. I can see your mainspring through there." She looked around and spied a small knife at Grobbin's belt. It was gaudily decorated with golden wings around the hilt and a glinting red gem set at the base. She slid it between armored cracks. "I now have it wedged so that if you even think about screaming, I will twitch a tiny bit and snap it. I don't know if you'll die or just be unable to move for a long time, but I'm betting you don't want me doing that. Now, squeak pathetically once if you understand me."

Grobbin squeaked. Once.

Matt sidled over to her, stuffing documents in his pockets as he did. "Wait, I'm supposed to be the fascist here?"

She shrugged. "I'm a quick learner. Be flattered. Besides, it's more fun being Bad Cop. What have you got there?" She pointed to the papers Matt was still holding out and studying.

"Orders for a team to go out and retrieve a corpse. Trusted prisoners under guard will be escorted to the site of the death..."

"Great, we don't look like prisoners... too fat and too tall. That won't work... let's see if Fuehrer Fuzzy here can help us..." She gave the key a half turn. Grobbin animated suddenly and opened his mouth. Bobbi interrupted him.

"Look and listen, Herr Chimpenstein. I can see how you work and I can take you apart. So don't do anything we don't want you to do. She twisted *something* inside his back, and his left arm twitched spasmodically in response. She removed the key. "I figure you've got about thirty seconds of run time. So we need you to tell us how to get out of here..."

"You can't escape. Surrender, and I might take your cooperation into..."

"Blah, blah, confess and we'll go easy, blah, blah. God, do all of you sturm-and-drang types study from the same playbook? Look, we're getting out of here somehow, and the only issue is how many pieces I leave you in when we..."

The door opened. Two guards were there, ducking slightly to get their tall hats under the low door.

"Warden, we..." They stopped when they saw the situation and began to draw their guns.

Bobbi said, quickly, "Freeze, or your boss goes 'sproing' all over the place!"

Grobbin, feeling the knife twist on his mainspring, just said, "Do it."

Bobbi smirked. "Okay, come inside... slowly... and shut the

door."

They did, watching her and Matt carefully.

Bobbi looked at them. "The one on the left's about my size..."

"Wow. It worked."

Bobbi looked around the bluish forest. The prison was a good mile or so behind them. Two prisoners accompanied them, their faces expressionless and dull. Bobbi turned and looked down towards one.

"Run. Go. Leave."

Matt sidled up next to her, whispering, "Huh? We don't know what they've done."

"You saw what that place was like! No one deserves that," she hissed back.

"For all we know, this is the munchkin Jeffrey Dahmer!" Then he stopped. "No. No, you're probably right. That was minimum security, overall. It's probably okay. Besides, I couldn't live with myself." He likewise turned to the prisoners. "Go. Run."

They stood still.

"What's wrong? You're free. Make your escape. Go on, scoot!"

One just shook his head.

"Trying to escape is a special offense. How stupid do you think we are?" The other nodded, then added, "So where's the poor fool who did try it? We have to haul him back, right?" There was something terrible about the squeaky, high-pitched voices speaking in tones of bitter, resigned, defeat.

Bobbi, meanwhile, was starting to undo her uniform, struggling with the complex brass buttons. "Look, we're not... damn, how do you people manage to take showers? ... really guards! We're... uh... spies! We're escaping... you can, too!"

There was quick buzz of conversation. Then one, the slightly taller one with wisps of brown hair, said, "Fine. Hand us your guns."

"Why?" said Matt, who had mostly managed to get his suit adjusted.

"So you can't shoot us in the back. If you're really leaving, you won't need them."

Bobbi glanced around. "We have a long way to go. What if there's animals in the woods? Lions..." She let her voice trail off as

Matt handed his pistol, grip first, to the speaker.

"Here. Good luck. "

The small man reached out for it carefully, as if it was made of burning metal. He then snatched it quickly and checked the chamber. He looked back at Matt with astonishment mixed with deep suspicion.

"Who do you work for? Really?"

"You know those Kansas Men? They're criminals. I'm a policeman from Kansas. I'm here to track them down."

The munchkin rolled his eyes. "Yeah, right. Look, thanks for the gun, I guess you don't need to tell me who you are." He smiled. "Only little kids and idiots believe in Kansas."

"Fine. Whatever. Look, I do have one small favor… do you know where the Kansas men come from? I mean, when they show up at the prison, they have to be coming from somewhere, right? Do you know where?"

The second one, the quieter one, spoke up now. "East of the prison. I saw it once. A small place. Not far from here."

Matt nodded. "Guarded?"

"I saw two men, dressed like you are now, with small guns." He held aloft the massive pistol the guards carried. Matt pondered that just about anything, even a .44 Desert Eagle, would be a "small gun" next to that thing. It didn't fill him with confidence.

"Can you show me which way?"

The ex-prisoner nodded and pointed. "About half a mile. Good luck." His partner was tugging at him. An alarm was beginning to sound, faint at this distance, but audible.

Bobbi looked in the direction of the sound. "Looks like they finally found Grobbin and the guards." She glanced at the key she still held. "I think this is dead as a bargaining chip." She tried bending it, and found it was surprisingly sturdy. "That was anti-climactic. Hm." There was a small hole in the ground, probably for a gopher. She shrugged and tossed the key into it, and was rewarded with a stream of noise that sounded like very fast, very descriptive profanity. The key came flying back out again. She picked it up again.

"Souvenir, I guess."

The two ex-prisoners had fled. Matt had managed to pull his suit back into position, though it was definitely showing signs of strain from their adventures. "Our best bet is towards that 'place where the Kansas men come from.'"

"Fine. Let's hope they're not on alert, too."

"Alarm's barely audible here. If they're further away... well, we have to risk it. Come on."

In the clearing was a large hot air balloon. Not a modern vacuum blimp, but an old fashioned, gasbag style balloon, seemingly without any kind of engines or other controls. There was a scattering of buildings – a Quonset hut and a few aluminum sheds, and three men wearing the overly ornate uniforms typical of the locals.

There were several other men striding purposefully about the small complex, two of which exhibited body language and demeanor that screamed "Fed" to Matt's highly trained eye... especially since he recognized one of them from his office building back on Prime. He watched as with pained resignation as Jason Watson from Narcotics went into the hut. The other man, the one he didn't know, was talking to one of the uniformed guards. The second guard began adjusting the ropes on the balloon, and the third...

The third was walking towards Bobbi and Matt.

Bobbi looked at Matt questioningly, gesturing to ask him what they were supposed to do. Matt shrugged. The guard walked close to them, then turned and began the somewhat laborious process of undoing his belt.

Bobbi rolled her eyes. Matt sighed, and then focused his attention on the gun the guard had strapped to his waist. He looked back at Bobbi and pointed towards the gun belt, and then Bobbi looked back at him with confusion. Then he realized the guard had completed dropping his trousers, and then pointed down to the ground, where the gun was still visible amidst the pile of cloth. Then Bobbi smiled.

She reached for a large, heavy, branch. He did likewise. He gestured a countdown... one... two...

Bobbi didn't wait for three, but took the opportunity to strike at an exposed and sensitive target. The guard was inhaling to scream when Matt's branch took him in the gut. He staggered back and tripped over the tangle of his pants. Bobbi then dropped down, grabbed him, and put her hand over his mouth, while Matt struggled to create a quick gag and then tie the guard in the remnants of his uniform. He also took the gun.

Back at the clearing, Jason had returned from the Quonset hut, and was now wearing a dull grey suit with a dull brown tie, as well as a not particularly stylish hat. The other man, the unknown one, had vanished for the moment – perhaps to change as well. The two guards were talking to Jason, and one pointed into the woods. Jason frowned and looked intensely into the forest, but did not approach.

Matt checked out the gun. Standard Oz issue, it seemed. Red and gold in color, larger and heavier than the guns he was used to, oversized barrel. It was a revolver, with seven chambered bullets. Clean, well maintained. He hefted it experimentally, tried to get used to the weight and estimate the kick.

A harsh whisper came from Bobbi. "How come you get the gun?"

"I spend two hours a week at the range. How about you?"

"Um... fifth place in the Washington Women's Fragfest Invitational?"

"If we find a rocket launcher, it's all yours. For now... we're not trying to kill anyone. Just hijack the balloon. We... what are you doing?"

Bobbi had produced her cell phone and was adjusting it, peering through the viewfinder. "Documenting. This thing's got a great zoom function."

"Umm, well, yes, that's a good idea, but maybe you should document the balloon landing site, not the bound soldier?"

She shrugged. "I know what the people who read my blog like." Nonetheless, she also captured some images of the clearing. "I don't get it... one hot air balloon in the middle of nowhere?"

"I have a theory..."

"It could be bunnies?"

Matt stared at her.

"Never mind. What's your theory?"

"There may be... weak spots between worlds here, sort of natural Bridges. The math allows for them. Perhaps this is one such place, a convenient hole between realities."

Meanwhile, the two men were growing impatient. They had changed into nearly identical dull grey and brown suits, distinguished only by a slight difference in collar width. Jason gestured at his watch, and the woods.

One of the guards called out loudly: "Smedley! Private Smedley, be done with your business and get back here! Time is wasting!" Matt and Bobbi were silent, assessing the situation. When no answer came after thirty seconds, both guards looked at each other, nodded, then drew their guns and began to cautiously walk towards the treeline.

Matt slipped behind the largest tree he could find; Bobbi did likewise, clinging to her makeshift club. The guards approached. Matt waited, muscles tensed, then leapt out and grabbed the nearest one, placing the gun to his head as best he could. The long barrel did a lot to mess up his form; he realized that, if he fired, he'd graze the skull at best. Still, the grabbed man seemed reasonably compliant under the circumstances.

"Drop it. Drop the gun. You too!" Matt tried to gesture with the gun, which only made positioning it worse.

The second guard looked at the first for confirmation. The first, feeling cold (albeit cheerfully painted) steel pressing against his head, nodded frantically.

The gun hadn't made it to the ground before Bobbi grabbed it and smiled. "Pretty." she said, turning it over in her hands.

Matt tried to retain outward composure, but winced inwardly. *Please*, he thought. *Please let her have actually fired a real gun once in her life*. Contrary to what the occasional nut job liked to spew, firing guns in a video game no more made you a crack shot than playing football in a video game made you a quarterback.

Matt turned his attention to the two momentarily stymied guards. "Okay. We've got your guns. I'm going to let you go, and you're going to put your hands up and walk very slowly back towards the clearing. Okay?"

The guards nodded.

When the four of them emerged from the woods, they were met at first with disbelief and then with a sort of contemptuous anger. Jason looked at Matt.

"Anders? What the hell? We heard... well, nothing. What are you doing here?" There was an implication of "when we were told you'd been killed back at the prison," to his sentence, but he seemed to be unsure if Matt had recognized him back there and was trying to keep all options open.

"Just following orders. Glen told me to look into something, and it led me here."

The other man, the older one, frowned. "Glen did, huh? Well. I'll need to talk with him when I get back." He nodded. "So what's your game? You want in? You want a cut? Fine. You're obviously smart enough to get this far; I figure we can work something out. Give those poor shmucks back their guns, and we'll talk terms." He paused, then looked at Bobbi as if seeing her for the first time. "Who's the chick?"

Oh boy, thought Matt. That's going to cost him. Nonetheless, he continued his bluff, while trying to somehow signal to Bobbi that shooting wasn't going to be the answer here.

"If I'm smart enough to get here, break into that prison, and break out again, I'm smart enough not to trust you to split the pie any more ways than it has to be."

The older man shrugged. "Fair enough. Let's try it this way: If you let us go, drop the guns, and run very fast, you might get lost enough here in Candyland that we won't find you. You keep on with this, though, and you're both very, very, dead."

Matt sighed. "I know. I don't know what I'm getting mixed up in. This is too big for me. Heard it all before." He smiled. "But, you know, I've been looking for something big. I didn't sign up to chase down nerds. I signed up to do some good. Now I've got the chance. You think I'm going to back off?"

Jason snorted. "Very pretty, Anders. Been rehearsing?"

"A bit. I figured this part would come eventually. Now, why don't the two of you stand aside? Come on, over there."

He pointed to the balloon, then to Bobbi. "Get in. Start undoing the ropes."

Matt waited until she was in, then began getting into the balloon himself, constantly maneuvering to keep the gun pointed at the two men. Then he clambered in himself, somewhat clumsily, as he didn't want to give them even a moment's opening. They were clearly tensing to move as soon as they felt they were out of the direct line of fire.

He untied the last rope, and the balloon began to ascend. As soon as it was free, the four in the clearing began to race for the Quonset hut. As they did, Bobbi raised her own gun and fired. The older man, the one Matt never learned the name of, screamed and fell, clutching his ankle. Bobbi cursed and rubbed her hands.

"Ow! That *hurt!*"

"It's called 'recoil.' And what the hell did you do that for? Why shoot him?"

She sneered. "'Who's the chick?'" she said mockingly.

"You don't kill someone because they're not politically correct!"

"I didn't kill him. I shot him in the ankle. He'll be fine. Probably. Umm. Do they have any kind of weird infections in Oz?"

"I don't know."

She shrugged. "Ah, well. Hope springs eternal."

"That's not the point. They'd surrendered... well, they were disarmed, at any rate. You don't shoot unarmed men!"

"They were running for that hut, probably to get guns and shoot us down. I delayed them. Besides..."

"Besides what?" Matt looked down. Sure enough, the two guards had retrieved rifles and were aiming them skyward. Matt silently urged the balloon to climb faster. A wind was picking up, a dull roar starting to build.

"Besides, *you* may finally be living out your dream of being Dirty Harry, but me? I've had my apartment ransacked and my name flashed on national TV as a wanted fugitive. And, one way or another, both of those guys down there were at least a little bit responsible. I'm entitled to a bit of payback."

"You'll get it when this is over! We'll crack this, turn them in..."

"If we live. If you're right about what's going on. If this balloon doesn't dump us in the middle of the Gobi or the Pacific or... hey! They're shooting at us!"

Bullets were, indeed, whizzing by, and Matt was suddenly aware of just how not-made-of-Kevlar the envelope of the balloon was. The wind continued to build, and it was getting harder to hear Bobbi speak.

"...just saying... we die... hit one of..."

Then the wind took away all sounds, and soon, all light. Matt glanced down and saw nothing but swirling mist, dust, and greyness. *It's not possible*, he thought. *We didn't ascend that high, that fast.* The ground should have still been trivially visible, and the bullets should have been whizzing past...

When he had taken the Bridge which put him here, there was a quick, sudden, sensation, almost unnoticeable, a tiny feeling like walking through a wall of rice paper, so quickly overwhelmed by the nausea following the jump that he'd barely registered the experience. But now he was feeling it again, but slowly. He was passing through an invisible membrane, feeling it stress and strain against him. The grey, whirling mist began to sparkle and glow, brilliant bits of light exploding around him. Breathing was becoming difficult; his thoughts were likewise fogging, descending into a chaotic muddle. He had a dim sensation of falling, of his knees buckling, of his head smacking into the basket...

And then there was nothing but the wind.

And then there was sunlight.

And pain.

And something warm.

Matt slowly opened his eyes, to confront what seemed to be a blue hill. As memory and reason slowly returned, he realized it was Bobbi's thigh. He placed his hands beneath him and tried to lift himself, fighting back the dizziness and a near crippling headache.

Bobbi mumbled.

Matt shoved himself back, so he was sitting upright, leaning against the basket of the balloon. Bobbi, freed of his weight, curled up in pain and continued to mumble. Matt tried to make sense of it.

"I…uh… don't think we can shut off the sun."

A single grunted word was her only reply: "Shit."

He reached for the rim of the basket and heaved himself to standing. A green checkerboard sprawled below him. Far below him. A voice came from somewhat less far below him. "So… now… what? And… where are we? What happened?"

Matt tried to think through the pain. "Second question first… I think… we passed through a, a natural Bridge. Probably they form pretty regularly here. It looked like they got to come and go as they please."

Bobbi digested this. "Huh. Makes sense. I mean, the numbers ought to hold. My BATS friends would go nuts, especially Katie. She's really into the physics of it all. "

"You aren't? It's your job!"

Bobbi looked at him with what she hoped was a world-weary expression, weakened somewhat by the small stream of drool she felt running down her chin. She wiped it off. "No, it's not. It's how I commute to work. I love all the places the Bridges go, but I'm really not an expert in how they work. How do you know so much about them, anyway? This is your first trip."

"They're how my work commutes to *me*."

"Clever." She pulled herself to her feet and looked down. "So, about that *first* question…"

"Uh… if we were the guys who knew what they were doing, we'd look for something down below, and then carefully deflate and drop." He peered over the rim, hoping that "something" would instantly draw his attention to it. Nothing did.

There was a long pause. Then. "And since we're not them?"

"Still working on that."

Bobbi groaned again. "So glad I shot the pig when I had the

chance." She then flung her arm over her eyes and dropped back into the basket, to try to turn her eyes away from the sunlight.

Matt studied the balloon's limited set of controls. The technology seemed very basic, though the construction was new. A burner heated air, which lifted the balloon. A few valves controlled the intensity of the burner. In theory, cooling the air would cause the balloon to drop...

Everywhere below them was prairie or farmland, but on the horizon was a grey smudge of a city. Maybe a few miles east of them? If that was the nearest city, it was probably the center of all this mess. So then...

Wincing as he moved, Matt twiddled the valves. One caused the flames to burn hotter. He turned it the other way, and the flames diminished, then sputtered and died completely. Frantically, he turned it back, but there was no resumption of fire, just a faint hiss of gas.

The balloon began to descend.

He reached down, grabbed Bobbi's arm, and yanked her to her feet. She cursed, then looked at the non-existent flame and the rapidly approaching ground.

"What did you do?"

He forced a weak half smile. "Tried to land."

"Overachiever, aren't you? Shit." She looked at the mechanism. "Pilot light's out. We need a flame. Do you smoke?"

"No. You?"

"No."

"Great. We'll be the first people in history to die from *not* smoking."

Then he looked at the gun.

"We might... we might be able to get a spark by shooting this near the gas..."

Bobbi looked at him with a mixture of confusion and admiration. "You're insane. I like that."

Standing as far back as he could, given the small size of the basket, and closing his eyes, Matt fired. The gun thudded sharply into his hand; the recoil was more than he was expecting. Then there was a welcome rush of heat and the roar of flame.

Meanwhile, the ground had become awfully close.

Bobbi examined the balloons controls. After a few seconds, she said, "Okay. I think this will *slowly* turn down the flame. We need to have a controlled descent. Be nice if we knew where we were."

"At a guess, Kansas." Matt watched the ground stop rushing upwards with some relief. "Here's what I think happened. There's some kind of, I don't know, pan-dimensional jet stream that picks up right where we were. So that gives them a way to move back from Oz to this world's Earth, a link no one outside their little circle knows exists."

Bobbi nodded. "And, somehow, Loko hitched a ride, or stole a balloon, or something, and made it here… and from here back to Prime, where he wound up with Frank. And your people…"

"They're my coworkers, not my 'people.'"

"One of your coworkers figured out Frank had him. So they used me to tip you off to Frank, so the whole thing would look like it was coming from the outside."

"I'm not sure they knew about Loko. I think they just wanted to find out what Frank knew. The way Brian acted… he was surprised to see that munchkin. He over-reacted, and they covered it up as quickly as they could, then shut up Frank. Damn."

"So the key is figuring out how and where Loko got through to Prime."

"And surviving our landing." Matt looked down. The ground was passing below them at a moderate pace. "It's pretty much all flat here, but it looks like suburban sprawl is starting in a few miles. I don't think we want to crash in anyone's back yard."

Bobbi turned back to the valves. "This won't be smooth."

Matt rolled his eyes. "What has been?"

It wasn't really a crash, per se. More of series of scraping thuds as the slowly deflating balloon bounced along someone's dried up cornfield. The basket scraped along the ground with each impact, until it eventually tore itself to pieces and dumped Bobbi and Matt into the dry, grey, soil. Then ended up a few feet from a grievously underemployed scarecrow, which utterly failed to offer them directional advice, or, really, do more than hang limply.

Wincing, Matt got to his feet. He held out a hand to Bobbi, but she was already standing. A battered wooden fence was visible through the papery leaves, and beyond that was a road made of gravel and dust. When they reached it, they could see a low skyline ahead of them, and a battered sign read 'Topeka 5'.

Bobbi seemed to deflate. “Another walk. On gravel. Gah.”

Matt made his way back to the remains of the balloon. A toolbox in the basket had held various supplies – ropes, a flare gun, a compass. He emptied it out and placed the guns inside. Hopefully, he thought, they won’t be needed… but better to be safe,

It seemed to be late August here, and the sun battered them with the enthusiasm of a cop who was sure no one had a video camera in the vicinity. At the two-mile mark, the road shifted from gravel to asphalt, but by that point, every footstep was already excruciating. Matt dimly tried to ponder when he’d last slept… his last meal was a good ten hours before…

The two of them had taken a few minutes rest, perched on a roadside rock. Then there was a sudden noise, and a cloud of dust. Something was coming up the road. Desperately, Bobbi leapt up and raised her thumb in what she hoped was a universal gesture. *With my luck,* she thought*, here it will mean ‘I wish to commit seppuku by car. Please hit me at top speed.’*

The car slowed down gratifyingly, then, as it got close, suddenly sped up. The couple driving it had flashed Bobbi a look of utter contempt.

“Huh? I thought for sure they were going to stop. Jerks.”

“It might be the way you… er… we’re dressed.”

Bobbi glanced at herself. Jeans, loose t-shirt, sneakers, ammo belt of gadgets. “What’s wrong with the way I’m dressed?” She considered. “I mean, I could be cleaner, but we’re wandering lost by the side of the road! For all they know, we’ve been in a horrible accident and we have a… a… starving baby trapped in the burning wreckage of our car! Or something.”

“I think it’s more the amount of skin. Bare arms, tight jeans…”

She rolled her eyes. “Trust me, I could be a hell of a lot sluttier.”

“All relative. Judging from the suits we saw back at the clearing, this world’s still pretty conservative.”

Bobbi snarled, then began walking again, trying not to wince with each step. “And what was up with that car, anyway?”

“It looked pretty old fashioned, true… but it’s hard to separate style from sophistication. Best not to make assumptions.”

They trudged on.

The world wasn’t in black and white, but, thought Bobbi, it might as well have been. Topeka was the dullest city she had seen, duller than she had ever imagined a city could be. Though the newspaper said it was 2008, it seemed that technology here was barely out of the 1930s. No color photographs, and even where color was used in ads, it was dull and muted. As they walked, drawing a lot of angry stares and harsh whispers, Bobbi searched desperately for some signs of life. Women were dressed so that the only skin showing was that of their face... even in the harsh summer heat, gloves and long skirts were the only allowable fashion. Men, too, dressed in three-piece suits, except for the laborers, who tended to wear uniform jumpsuits straight out of some failed Eastern bloc nation. Even Matt's dowdy FBI suit looked positively exotic and daring.

I do not like this place, she thought. *Judging from the looks I'm getting, it doesn't like me. And I'm hungry.*

"We need food. And water. And, I guess, new clothes."

"Which means we need local money."

Bobbi looked back at him. "You've got that cash from Brian."

"Not much. It didn't go that far in Oz. I've got..." He counted "...12 bucks. I don't know what that will buy here, but I'm guess it's not much. We need more and I'd rather get it now."

Matt looked around, then tapped Bobbi's arm and gestured. There was a pawn shop. "Got anything you can sell? I doubt we'll find the kind of currency exchange we did in Oz."

She made a show of patting down her pockets. "Nothing that would be legal to sell... and I'm sort of traveling with a cop. Everything I'm carrying could do a major Connecticut Yankee on this place. If they could even make sense of it..."

"Great. I've got a class ring and..." He sighed and slapped his head. "A pile of Oz coins. All precious metals. Those sell everywhere."

Matt had never before encountered a pawnshop owner who asked so many questions. Most preferred to maintain a firm wall of plausible deniability, but this one was so inquisitive that Matt was tempted to hand him a job application. After a hastily fabricated story about a "nutty uncle Frank" who liked to mint coins to give as gifts, Matt was able to sell the assorted pieces of gold and silver for what he suspected was far less than their actual value.

Then came the rather nightmarish experience of buying appropriate clothes. Matt found it fairly trivial to find a dull grey suit and a dull brown tie. Bobbi, however, was more reticent.

“None of this stuff looks decent!” she whispered to him harshly, in the third clothing store they’d tried.

“I didn’t think you cared about how you dressed...” Matt began, and then trailed off. Somewhere, he knew, there must be a universe where looks could, indeed, kill. He was very glad this wasn’t it.

After a minute of cold silence, he tried again. “Look, we’re trying to blend. Just pick something that matches what other women are wearing.”

“Great. A thrilling choice between dowdy pale blue and dowdy pale grey. Not to mention gloves, an ankle length skirt, and a hat my octogenarian aunt wouldn’t wear because it’s too frumpy.”

“A seasoned Bridge traveler such as yourself must be used to odd local customs.”

She sneered. “*Cool* odd local customs. *Fun* odd local customs. I bridge to see interesting places, not dumps like this.”

Matt glanced at his watch, hoping that no one else was looking closely enough to see how anachronistically advanced it was. “It’s past six. The store is closing soon, we’ve been walking most of the day, and I don’t know about you, but I’m exhausted. We need to find a place to eat, and then... a hotel. Oh, and a local paper. Let’s see what kind of world this is.”

The restaurant was labeled simply “Cookies,” and consisted of a lunch counter and a handful of small wooden tables. A bored waitress led them to one such, and tossed down two small pieces of paper. Bobbi glanced at one of them quickly, and then called the waitress back.

“Hey, sorry to be a pain, but can we see the full menu?”

The waitress’ mood visibly shifted from boredom to annoyance.

“Whaddya mean? That’s what we got. If you don’t like it, tough.”

“Um... but there’s only, like, about ten things on here. All which seem to involve a dead animal and way too much starch.”

Matt rubbed his head, and swore to himself that the next time he was running across dimensions being chased by members of his own organization, he’d recruit someone who knew what ‘keeping a low profile’ meant.

The waitress sneered. “What, you got allergies or something?”

“No, it’s just... I mean... why so few items?”

“We serve what everyone serves. This is what people like. *Normal* people.”

“Fine, fine... um... cheeseburger. What kinds of cheeses do you have?"

"American."

"Yes, and...?"

"What else do ya want?"

"Fine. Just... fine. Cheeseburger."

"Lovely." The waitress made a rapid scrawl on her pad. "And you?"

"Uh... meatloaf, I guess."

The waitress walked away with their orders, shaking her head and wondering why she got stuck with all the weirdoes.

Matt began reading through the paper. The majority of the stories were useless tedium containing very little news of other nations, or even of other states. The local dominated utterly. This was a world where few people traveled far, it seemed, or cared about what happened elsewhere.

No comics, either.

He noticed Bobbi's lips moving. He closed up the paper, which drew an angry grunt from her. She grabbed it and flattened it out. There was something in the classifieds that had caught her attention.

"Look at this!" She tapped one small ad triumphantly.

"What?" Matt looked. It was a "Lost Or Missing" ad, noting that several radios were stolen, and asking if anyone had seen them. Each radio was followed by a serial number. "So? Radios. I figured they'd be at least that advanced."

She rolled her eyes. "No. Look! Look at the serial numbers!"

Matt looked. "4D45455449... What? I don't see anything."

Her voice dropped to a conspiratorial whisper. "ASCII Hex." When she saw the blankness in his eyes, she continued. "Data storage values. It's a computer code. Look: 'Meeting tonight. Lamont Hotel. Room 5G.'"

"Okay, it's a bit suspicious, but it's probably... just... local..." His voice trailed off. "They don't have computers here. Not with this level of technology."

She nodded. "And even if they did, the odds of them using the same code sequence... trust me on this, I do this for a living, remember?"

"The people running this wouldn't need to send each other secret messages via newspaper ads. So therefore..."

"Some other group here is aware of the Bridges." Bobbi finished his sentence for him, just as two plates were unceremoniously dumped in front of them.

"Frank's people?"

"Probably."

"We needed a hotel to stay at…"

They finished their meal quickly, paid, and left.

As they tried to locate the Lamont, Bobbi continued to complain about the food. "What the hell was wrong with that place? Even the hole-in-the-walls back home have four page menus. Hell, have you seen the newsstands here? There's like, five magazines on them. I only see maybe three or four models of car. Everything is so… so… constrained! Even allowing for the tech…"

"They're pretty cut off," Matt said. "From what I could pick up from the paper, there's very little foreign trade or contact. Some of the news items about what's happening overseas were a few weeks old. It looks like there's no transatlantic communication, other than by ship."

"But they've got telephones and radios."

"Technology and culture aren't the same thing. These people… well… they like to keep to themselves, it seems. A lot. Look, it's 2008 here, and it looks like they've advanced about as far as we did by the late 1920s. Based on what I know about alternate evolutions, that usually is a result of isolationism, and here, it was taken to extremes. Looks like they've cut themselves off from everything."

Bobbi stopped walking suddenly.

"What is it?"

"Bookstore. Come on, we've got to see what passes for literature around here!"

"Um… yeah… I suppose… look, uh…"

She rolled her eyes. "I promise not to bring anything back home."

The bookstore was small. Very small. An old man with thin glasses and a worn suit peered over the counter at them. "Can I, ah, help you?"

Bobbi bounced over to him. "Yeah! Where's the sci-fi?"

He blinked. "The, uh, what?"

"Science fiction? Fantasy?"

"Not, uh, sure what you mean. Science books are there, fiction's over there." He gestured towards two small shelving areas, each holding about two dozen books apiece.

Bobbi decided not to bother trying to explain further, but went to check out the fiction. There wasn't much, and what there was seemed to be both utterly dull and totally focused on the local culture. Not one book had a plot that didn't involve Kansas.

She went back to the bookseller, while Matt was intently studying some thick tome. "Um, don't you have any books not about Kansas?"

"Why would folks want to read about stuff like that? Folks like books they can relate to. "

Bobbi stormed over to Matt. "So much for my cunning plan of smuggling some books out of this backwater under your nose. There's nothing here worth taking back. C'mon."

Despite her being eager to leave, Matt insisted on purchasing the book he had been skimming, along with a few others.

"What were those?" she asked. "And you're surely not going to be importing them..."

"Histories, and no. I was right. This world's raised isolationism to an art form. From the looks of things, it's the only art form they practice. Here."

He handed her a thin paperback.

"What's this?"

"Like it says on the cover: A History Of The Arts. It's pretty thin, you'll notice."

"Yeah."

"No Shakespeare here. No Twain. Harold Robbins made it, though. That explains a lot."

"How does it explain no Swiss cheese for my cheeseburger?"

"Well... think about it. Back home, on Prime, you've got access to dozens of cultures and thousands of subcultures... and that's just the local population. When the Bridges opened 20 years ago, those numbers exploded. Now, no matter who you are or what you want, you can find other people like yourself, or just a steady stream of whatever it is you need. I mean, no matter how obscure your interest, there's always someone else who shares it... sometimes, a whole planet of someones."

Bobbi took another swig of soda. "Yeah. Like, you know, Furtopia."

Matt laughed. "Right. Here, though... they don't have the Bridges, sure, but they've barely got trade. Every nation locked away in its own little isolationist world. Even the States here are barely United. No wonder this world is so stagnant, so dead, so... grey." He paused. "Hell, I wonder if... Nah. Silly."

Bobbi nudged him in the elbow. "What?"

"Well... it's just... all that potential, locked away. All that imagination and creativity, denied a place to express itself... maybe Oz is here, on this world, because all of that had to... I don't know... go somewhere. All of the things no one here dared express or say, all the ideas, all the joy... had to find someplace else to exist."

Bobbi didn't laugh. Instead, she just said, with an oddly distant tone, "The third theorem on fictives."

Matt looked puzzled. She continued.

"You know the two main theorems... the Infinite Worlds theorem and the Inspiration theorem. Well, some people... mostly a bunch of nutters, if you ask me... have what they call the Third Theorem. They think we're reversing cause and effect. We on Prime aren't discovering fictive worlds or being inspired by them... we're creating them. We don't imagine them because they exist, they exist because we imagine them."

Matt snorted. "I'm sorry, but you're right. They *are* nutters. Even if I was sounding like one a minute ago."

Bobbi grinned wickedly. "Are they?" She stopped. "Here we are on a street corner. Do we go left or right?"

"Um... we're lost either way. So... left."

"Right!" she said. "No, not *go* right. Look. Basic reality theory says that somewhere else, you said 'right' just now instead of left. You've just made a world... a whole universe... by a simple decision. So if something as trivial as picking left or right makes a universe... what about the creation of a book or a movie or a TV show? If you can forge an entire reality without even trying, what about the people who *are* trying?"

Matt blinked and considered. "That's just... I mean... how would you prove it?"

Bobbi smiled. "You can't. And that's part of the beauty of it all. Even with everything we've got, even with entire universes serving as nothing but tourist traps, there's always going to be something new to learn. Such as, for example, the location of the hotel."

Six stories tall and made of red brick, the Lamont was one of the more aesthetically appealing buildings they'd seen, though the local competition wasn't too stiff. A wide, marble-floored lobby and uniformed doormen awaited them. There were a few splashes of color here, more than there usually were – gold trim on the counters, a bright red carpet, and a gaggle of blue-uniformed police at the front desk.

"Shit." said Matt, as he began pulling Bobbi back out of the lobby.

"What? We haven't done anything wrong here."

"They're looking for us."

"What, do you have cop-dar or something? Maybe a guest got his luggage snatched or whatever. What gives you the idea they're after us?"

"That." Matt said, pointing to the WANTED poster featuring their faces.

"Oh."

They ducked around the hotel and into a convenient alley.

"Why the hotel? How could they have guessed we'd be there?"

"They knew we had no contacts here. They knew we'd need a place to stay. Contrary to what you think, the people I work with aren't idiots."

"Just criminals and murderers."

"Um… yeah. I'm losing this one, aren't I?"

"Oh yeah. Big time."

Matt thought for a moment. "On the other hand…"

"What?"

"Well... maybe they think we know more than we do. It's obvious Frank's been talking to these people. Maybe... maybe they assume we know them. That they're going to look for us here. Or not. We don't know if they know… hmm."

"Right, we can play this game all day. I'm getting bored. What are we going to do *now?*"

"Now…" he said, "We're going to that meeting. I am sick of all this speculation. I am going to find someone who has some clue what's going on, and hopefully doesn't want to kill me." He pointed to a fire escape. "Give me a boost."

"Yeah, right. You weigh about 60 pounds more than me. *You* lift *me* up."

Being both a gentleman and keen on surviving the next five minutes, Matt didn't dispute the presumed weight difference, but simply acquiesced, hoisting Bobbi to the point where she could clamber over the lowest terrace of the fire escape. She quickly undid the latch and sent the ladder dropping down. Matt clambered up.

"Room 5G. Let's climb."

The fifth floor window was closed, but unlocked. It took a few moments to pry it open and scramble inside.

"5K... 5J... here's 5G."

"Do you read out billboards as you drive past them?" Bobbi asked.

"Hmm?"

"It's just... that's one of the most annoying things in the world. People who feel they have to read signs out loud. It's something people do when they're in the car and they feel they have to make some kind of noise if there's anyone in there with them."

Matt paused for a moment, stumped. "I... umm... never notice. I usually drive alone..."

Bobbi nodded. "Probably yes, then." She paused. "Well?"

"Well what?"

"5G. Shouldn't you knock? Or are you trained mostly to kick down doors and start shooting, in case someone's carrying a fully loaded DVD player?"

"No, we knock first. *Then* we haul out the bazooka. That way, they're likely to be behind the door and blown to pieces when we fire. Standard protocol 12-B."

Matt watched as she parsed this and tried to decide if he was joking or not. Evidently, the scales tipped, ever so slightly, towards 'joking,' for she emitted a mirthless 'ha' and then gestured again to the door.

Matt knocked.

A voice from within said "Klaatu."

Matt blinked, then said, "Umm... hello? We're, uh, here for the meeting..." He could hear a scrambling inside, the familiar sound of contraband being hastily hidden.

Bobbi rolled her eyes "Barata Niktu" she said loudly, followed by, "Don't mind my friend, he's a bit slow sometimes."

Matt was about to speak, when the door opened. Matt expected someone scruffy, likely overweight, and wearing a t-shirt with either a logo or a witticism barely one percent of the populace would get. Instead, the man behind the door looked like he was a member of the local chapter of Junior Boring Middle Managers Of America.

He looked at the two of them with surprise and then suspicion.

"I don't think I know you."

Bobbi smiled. This seemed to have an effect on the young man behind the door. "We're from... uh... out of town." she said, deftly stepping past him as he tried to parse through the notion there was a reasonably attractive woman passing within mere inches of him without expressing any evident disdain or fear. “We saw the message in the paper, and figured we’d stop by. Come on in, Matt.”

The man closed the door quietly behind him. “Out of town…” His brow furrowed. “You wouldn’t know a man named Frank, would you? He was supposed to be here tonight…”

Bobbi nodded. “Yeah, I know him. He… couldn’t make it.”

Matt scanned the room. It was a typical hotel room, with two small twin beds, a desk which contained a phone with a dial on it, two nightstands, a narrow door which probably led to a bathroom, and a half a dozen earnest-looking young men in their early twenties, though they had the dress and bearing of men in their fifties. Hats were piled up on one of the beds. One of the men was pulling a box out from under a bed.

Door-opener was trying to adjust to a series of rapidly shifting paradigms. After a few seconds of working out what was going on, he finally held out his hand. “Well, hello then, I guess. I’m Ben, president of the Midwestern Scientifiction Appreciation Society.”

Matt took his hand and shook it. “And these are some of the local chapter?” he said, gesturing around at the other six people in the room. The group had formed a sort of half circle around Bobbi, who was looking through the box with an odd expression. The body language of the others was that of pack animals who were trying to figure out if the newcomer to their camp was friendly or would try to rip their throats out. *Good luck with that, boys,* thought Matt. *I still haven’t quite worked it out.*

Meanwhile, Ben was still speaking. “Um… actually, this is almost all of them.”

“All of the Topeka chapter?”

“All of the Society.”

“Oh.”

“We’re only a year old, of course. It’s hard to find members.”

There was a sudden cry from the other side of the room.

“That bastard! He told me he’d returned this! This is *my* book, dammit!”

Bobbi was waving around a paperback. “First edition Ringworld! With Earth going backwards! I loaned it to him so he could ‘archive’ it, and when I asked where it was he made some big song and dance about how he’d given it back to me and he saw me take it and maybe if I cleaned my apartment once in a while… ooooh! Like his place was any better. I’m going to…” She stopped, realizing her next words were going to be “kill him,” then continued. "Ah, I guess it doesn't matter that much. Damn."

Matt took a look in the box. Every book in there, an assortment of classic science fiction, seemed to be from Prime.

"Now that's weird."

"What is?"

"Well, Frank's hobby was smuggling books and media *into* Prime. Why is he... was he... bringing books out?"

Ben spoke.

"He... well, he came to me about a year back. I work, umm, I'm not supposed to discuss this, but if you're friends of Frank..." Bobbi and Matt each, in their own way, decided that 'friends' was a close enough approximation to their actual relationship, and nodded. *Nah, we're the ones who got him killed* didn't seem like a good way to get more information.

"Well, I work for the War Department." Ben continued. "We're working on a sort of... I guess you'd call it an electric adding machine. It's a bit more than that, of course, but it's awfully hard to explain..." He had the eager look of one desperate to explain more. Bobbi swatted that down.

"A computer. Probably the first this hellhole has seen. Go on."

The way his face fell was almost painful to watch.

"Umm... yes. Well, Frank was looking for... books of this type... from here. From, uh, this world, I guess you'd say."

Matt nodded. "And he couldn't find any."

"Nothing... nothing recent. There's some very old books by Defoe, Voltaire, Walpole, and the like, which were close to what he was looking for... but a lot of the other names he gave us, well, Wells was a historian, and a pretty dull one, Verne was a lawyer and a politician, and the others... Campbell, Lovecraft... we never heard of them at all."

"And so he decided to import some."

"Yeah... they've been... I mean, the ideas... there's so much to absorb. It's hard sometimes to sort out what's real and what's fantasy... so much of your world seems unreal to me, it's fantastic enough. "

"Hmm. Never thought of it that way."

Ben seemed astonished. "But... but... I mean... you travel across dimensions!"

Matt sighed. "It was pretty spectacular when it started. But that was twenty years ago. Now, its just... part of the scenery." He sat down on the bed. "I mean, I tell women at parties that my job is tracking down inter-reality copyright violations, and they just yawn and walk away and go look for a stockbroker with a great big... portfolio or something."

Ben's eyes narrowed. "So you're not Frank's friend."

Matt winced inwardly. *I keep forgetting that 'backward' and 'stupid' aren't the same thing.* "Okay, no, I mean, I wasn't, that's how this mess all started... I was investigating him, but not for this... then..."

Bobbi interrupted quickly. "Let's get to the point. Where did the munchkin come into all this?"

Ben turned to her. "You know about that? Frank said it had to be kept secret until the time was right... until he knew everything..."

Matt looked back at him. "Frank won't be knowing anything, anymore. He's dead. He was killed because he was on the verge of finding out what was going on. We've been piecing it together. You're part of it."

"You mean Loko."

"Yes. Loko."

Another one of the young men spoke up. "That would be my doing. I'm Thomas, by the way. I found Loko out by my farm."

Matt gestured for him to continue.

"It was about a month ago, just before our last meeting. There was a storm, a nasty one, with twisters setting down. I was out rounding up the cows -- trying to get them inside the barn -- when everything went... rainbowey, I guess is the word. There was a cyclone coming down real fast, whipping up out of nowhere right in front of me, but it was weird, all shining lights and colors and a noise like, well, like nothing I'd ever heard. Then it blew away, and there was this little boy left on my field.

"Except it wasn't a little boy, it was a man... a tiny man, and he looked like hell. He was talking nonsense, or what I thought was nonsense, all about monkeys and magic and prison and so on. I didn't know what to do, so I brought him inside and gave him some food. I was going to call the police to come and help him, but he panicked when I said that. I admit I was a little scared, maybe he was some kind of escaped criminal, but I figured, what could a little starving fellow do to me?

"I eventually got him calmed down enough to get him to make some sense... well, sense only because I'd met Frank and knew about these 'alternate worlds' and such. He came from one, too, a weird one, with little people and witches and flying monkeys and such. It seemed maybe Frank would know what to do, I brought him along."

Bobbi interrupted. "I'm going to guess the rest. Frank saw him and practically had an orgasm at discovering some oppressed proletariat he could get the credit for aiding, and convinced him to come on back to our world. Right?"

Thomas looked both pained and confused by the analogy, but nodded. "Yes... we found a steamer trunk, and Frank has us help him rig up a false bottom..."

"He was a pretty good smuggler." Matt noted.

"So he went back through the Bridge, you people call it, with Loko, and that's the last we saw of him."

Matt sighed. "My people, in turn, knew or suspected something, and set the gears in motion, trying to make it all look like it came from outside. But why hide him? Why not bring it all out at once?"

"Showmanship." snorted Bobbi. "If he'd just trotted Loko out to a press conference, it would have turned into a mess of he said, they said, and by the time a formal investigation had begun, Frank would only be a footnote. He wanted it all, he wanted to be the hero, and so he was biding his time while he worked out the details. Remember, he had the coordinates for the prison camp on his system. He was probably planning some kind of showy raid with a couple dozen of his activist friends and a whole bunch of cameras. Never got to pull it off. Stupid bastard."

"Can I safely assume you're recorded most of this?"

Bobbi tapped her phone. "Of course."

"Then I think we've got enough. Just get back through this Bridge and we're home free."

There was a harsh knock on the door.

"Topeka Police! We're just checking for some fugitives who might be here. Please open the door."

Matt rushed to the window, looked down. Five stories to the street. Worse still, this room had a wonderful view of the city, rather than dingy back alley, and there was not a pile of trash bags or a convenient dumpster in sight.

"Damn." He went for the basket. He didn't really want to shoot a cop, who was almost certainly convinced he was tracking down dangerous criminals, but the alternative was likely to be his own life...

As he held the gun, pondering, the door burst inwards. The

sound of breaking wood was quickly followed by the sound of shattered porcelain, as Bobbi smashed one of the hotel lamps against the intruding officers face. He staggered back, blood from numerous small lacerations streaking his face, and fumbled for his gun. Matt leapt over the bed, grabbed the cops arms, pulled him forward and down, and elbowed him in the back of the skull. He collapsed.

There was no one else in the hall. Probably they'd split up to canvass the hotel, but this one would be noticed soon. The six others in the room were staring in various degrees of shock.

"We're leaving by the same fire escape we came in on. I recommend you boys do the same. They aren't after you, and if you're lucky, this guy didn't get a good look at you before Bobbi got him." He then turned to her. "You know, you like hitting cops a little bit too much."

She shrugged. "I haven't hit *you* yet."

"I'll take what comfort I can from that."

"And I didn't think there'd be so much blood!" she protested as they dashed down the hall.

"You hit a man with something that shatters into hundreds of tiny sharp pieces. What did you expect?"

"Uh… a little 'stunned' icon to appear over his head?"

The group had reached the window. Matt turned to the various club members. "Look, thanks for all your help. If it means anything, you may be stopping something very bad going on a long way away. Um… keep meeting. I'll… I'll see what I can do about sending some more stuff your way."

Bobbi laughed. "Planning on arresting yourself?"

"Just get down the fire escape. I'll have moral angst about my job sometime when we're not running from police, okay?"

As he prepared to exit the window, Ben thrust something into his hand. "This is my phone number. If you need to contact me…"

Matt took it absentmindedly. "Yeah, sure. Thanks. Good luck." He then began the scramble down the ladder.

There was a shout from the window. "Wait!" Matt glowered back at Ben.

"Look, really love to chat, but there's cops after us at the moment."

"And you'll need a place to hide. What plan did you have?"

Matt pondered for a second. "Planning hasn't been very high on my list in the past day or so. I have been, as the saying goes, making it up as I go along." Down below, Bobbi was alternately looking up at him, looking out the alley, and tapping her foot nervously. She gestured frantically. Finally, Matt realized she was saying "Stay up there if you want to, but send the guns down to me."

He looked back at Ben. "You're willing to take on fugitives? What about your security clearance?"

Ben shrugged. "So far, there's no connection between you and me, if we get away before the cops see us..."

"Fair enough." Matt started down the ladder; Ben followed. The remainder of the club did likewise, then scattered.

Matt looked around the alley. "We need to split for a bit, so no one sees us together. We'll meet at your house." He checked the address again. It read "79th Street," and Matt was sure he'd seen where 12th street was. Shouldn't be too hard to find. He nodded. Ben took off.

There was a wail of sirens.

Of course, there's the whole "wandering around the streets" problem...

He glanced back at the alley again, and found what he was looking for. He walked over to the grate and gave it an experimental tug. It was loose, but heavy. "A little help here?" he asked Bobbi.

She looked dubiously at the grate.

"Umm... what?"

"It's a sewer grate. We lift it, we go down into the sewers."

She glowered. "I know that. The question is 'why?'"

"Well, for starters, we're wanted, the hotel is about to be swarming with cops, and it's damn likely at least one will peek down this alley while we're talking. And I don't feel like wandering the streets while everyone is looking for us. No matter how backwards this place might be, some of my people are running the search. Furthermore, do you want to bet there's no ACLU here?"

"Sounds like your dream world," she snorted, but she also helped him lift the grate.

There was a ladder. Bobbi looked down. "'You are in a very dark place,'" she quoted. "'You may be eaten by a grue.'"

Matt tried to make sense of that, couldn't, and then headed down. Bobbi followed. While Matt had managed to get his feet onto the concrete ledge that ran along the sewer proper, Bobbi missed, and her feet landed in several feet of vile ooze.

I am going to write an adventure novel, she thought. I am going to discuss how much long walks make your feet hurt, and just how vile a sewer is. Every damn adventurer seems to spend half their time merrily trotting through these things, and they never really discuss the smell. Her dinner made a concerted escape attempt; she beat it back with the gusto of a guard at Alcatraz.

"So now what?" she whispered, as Matt helped her out of the ooze. She hoped, for his sake, that he wasn't smirking. If she had to kill him now, she'd be alone in this dreary world.

He looked around. "There's got to be markings on the walls here, so the workers can find their way around. We make our way to as close to 79th street as we can, we wait for dark, we come out, and we find Ben."

"Assuming he hasn't just, y'know, told all the cops we'll be at his place so he can get a fat reward."

"You have any other plans?"

"No," she finally admitted.

They began to walk.

"So what was with that 'dream world' crack?"

"Huh? Oh. I mean, wouldn't it make your job easier if there weren't people running around screaming about rights and laws and procedures? Don't you just want to whack people on the head and toss them in some dank pit for the rest of their lives?"

"If you mean people who are enslaving munchkins for drug farming… well, yeah, I'd like it to be as simple as just blowing them all away. But if you mean people like Frank… no."

"So then why do it? Why spend your days tracking down nerds?"

He sighed, not wanting to tell her how many times he'd asked himself that.

"Well, sometimes it's not just the collectors and the fans. You remember, about four years ago, the whole 'Jedi' thing?"

"The 'one year pre-release' mess?"

"Right. Now there's a case where some serious harm could have been done, where they had mastered and duplicated thousands of bootlegs of a movie that was still in post-production here."

"Yeah, but Frank never trafficked in that. He liked the stuff that had no parallels at all… the sequels never written here, that episode of the Twilight Zone that Lovecraft worked on… come on, you know you're not doing anything important there."

"Well, you've hit it, in a way. I'm at this job because I want to do something important… something good. Your friends the BATS…

they think weapons smuggling is just a big joke, and maybe it is when they're talking a milspec analytical engine or a... an armor plated zeppelin or whatever, but there's really dangerous stuff out there. Bioviruses. Moore's grass. Ice-9. Carnivorous tribbles."

She laughed, and then looked at him. "You're not kidding. Whoa."

"Yeah. We, uh, don't talk about that one too much. But it's all real." He took a breath. "I didn't sign up for nerd patrol, but that's where they stuck me, and I'm going to keep at it until I can find a way to get out and get somewhere important. Fugitive tracking, for instance. People who commit crimes on Prime and then escape over a Bridge, or off-worlders who hole up back home."

"You mean... become one of the people who's probably looking for us now."

He shrugged. "I never said my life was going to be free from painful irony."

They walked more. Bobbi suddenly spoke up. "Say... we didn't get a cyclone, did we?"

"Huh?"

"That guy... he said Loko fell out of a cyclone. That means he didn't steal a balloon."

Matt shrugged. "They may have been another way. Something we didn't know about. I'm not sure if it matters."

Bobbi looked like she wanted to keep talking about it, but couldn't think of anything to add.

They walked.

"Did you ever meet yourself?" Matt asked, suddenly.

"What?"

"You've done a lot more Bridging than I have. From what you've said about your job... I'm guessing you mostly go to the 1-Deltas, the close parallels. Ever meet yourself?"

She nodded. "Once. I mean, I probably could have several times, if I'd bothered, but only once did it really happen. I was meeting with their IT guy in this place where IBM hadn't bothered to invest in computers and EMCC totally took off... anyway, he said that when he was entering my data in he noticed they had a 'Roberta Sinderman' working for them, wondered if I wanted to meet her... this was an 'open' contact, they knew about the Bridges... a little backwards in computer tech, but they'd stumbled on some great fertilizers Prime never found, so trade was starting up... anyway, I thought it would be kind of cool to meet myself, not kinky like in all those pornos, and I did, and, well…"

"What?" Matt stepped deftly around a small mound of something better left unidentified.

"She wasn't my evil twin. More like my Boring Twin. Okay, this world was a bit more button-down than Prime… not as bad as this dump, but still… anyway, I wasn't expecting her to be Wild Party Girl or anything, but she was, was, this mousy little nothing from the secretarial pool. I stupidly suggested lunch to her and by the end of it I wanted to kill her. She was just so, so, not *me*."

"There's a lot of people who aren't you. Why get so mad?"

"Because she could have been me. Same DNA. Same raw potential. She just made a lot of stupid choices. It was painful. I mean, how would you feel if you found someone who was you, but some sort of drugged out hippie slacker version of you, rotting in jail?"

Matt pondered. "I'd feel good about the choices I made. It would be proof I made the right ones, and that who I am now was due to *me*, to my decisions, not to my DNA."

"Huh. I guess that's… a good way to look at it." She smiled. "Ah, but what if you met someone who was, I dunno, head of the FBI or something? Fascist-in-Chief? Wouldn't you feel bad, knowing you *could* have been him but weren't?"

Matt shrugged. "I'd chalk his success up to dumb luck and favoritism."

"Nicely syllogistic. So you basically always come out with 'I'm the best me I can be,' huh?"

"Pretty much. Thus far, it's worked. How is all your existential angst working out for you?"

"Fine, you win this one."

They walked.

"Aaannd… we're here." Matt gestured up. "Through there, and we're done."

There was still light creeping through the manhole cover, though it was dim. They waited until dark, and then carefully lifted the lid.

They seemed to be in another alley, one behind a somewhat ramshackle two-story building. Streetlights were sparse here, and what light there was illuminated a long row of low, squat, buildings lining a narrow street. Few people were about.

Matt checked the address, then the house numbers. They were about two blocks from Ben's place. Glancing down the street, Matt saw no obvious signs of a police ambush... then again, if the cops had any brains, the signs wouldn't be obvious.

"Shall we go?"

"Sure. Hopefully, this place has hot water. I could really use a shower. And some ice cream. Yeah. Lots of ice cream. And a chance to frag some llamas."

"You've got a shot at two out of three."

As they walked, they could not help but notice furtive glances from behind curtains. They tried to stay out of the light as much as possible, so, hopefully, the looks were simply due to this world's general distrust of anyone new, and not because there was a huge reward for their capture.

When they arrived at Ben's house, he practically pulled them through the door.

"Are you nuts? If you're running from the law, why are you wandering around after curfew? They'll grab you for that alone!"

"Curfew? Why? Is there a war? Some state of emergency?"

Ben seemed confused. "No... no war, at least not an American war, for over a century now. It's just... curfew. It keeps the streets safe."

Matt considered protesting this and decided against it. "Whatever. When in Rome, attend Bart's Orgy-O-Rama. So, this is your, uh, house."

The furnishings were spartan, but the clutter was something Matt had become all too familiar with. Books were scattered everywhere, along with papers. Stacks of loose paper were weighted down with random bits of machinery. Almost anything which could be written on, was. On the desk sat a manual typewriter, which was clearly in regular use, as it was one of the few items in the room that was not half-buried.

Bobbi glanced around, saw nothing of interest, and turned to Ben. "So, do they have showers in this backwater, or what?"

The Roberta Sinderman school of diplomacy, thought Matt, but Ben just pointed towards the back. She dashed in that direction, and a small squeal of excitement could be heard, followed by the whine of water rushing through the pipes.

"So... uh... can I get you anything?" Ben asked. "There's, umm, club soda... and water... and I could brew up some coffee, if you don't mind waiting..."

"Water, please." Matt suddenly realized how thirsty he was, and how tired. As Ben rummaged for glasses, Matt wandered towards the typewriter and glanced at the currently loaded page.

"Fire the atomic space guns!" shouted Space Captain MacGregor. "We'll blast those space pirates out of the ether, or Earth will be doomed!"

There was a shriek and a curse from the bathroom. A few seconds later, Ben emerged from the kitchen.

"It's, uh, just a little something I've been working on." Ben handed Matt a tall, thin, glass. There was a slightly sulfurous whiff to the water. "It's really not as good as the books Frank brought over, but..."

"Don't worry. It all starts about there. Who knows? You could be famous here, someday."

"Oh, no. I can't publish it. I mean, there's no real market here, and besides, it would probably violate the Wertham Act. It's just for me, and maybe some of my friends."

"Ah." Matt couldn't think of much to say after that, so he just sat down, shunting aside some more papers. These were covered with diagrams and notations. He looked at them intently.

"Your computer work?"

"Computer? Oh, you mean the Electric Calculator with Heuristic Operation. The ECHO."

"Not a bad acronym. It beats 'BATS.'"

"Hmm?"

"Never mind."

Bobbi emerged, wrapped in several towels. Ben turned the color of a ripe apple. "So. Solved all of our problems yet?"

"Not even started."

"Great. Well, we're out of hot water. Or we're in hot water. But not the good kind." She kicked some papers aside and sat down, ignoring the fact her hair was dripping on diagrams of what was this world's first small, timorous step into the information age.

"We need to get home." Matt said, suddenly.

Bobbi favored him with a look of perfected disdain. "I'm starting to see why you're still stuck in nerd patrol. I know that. Any ideas how? Both sides of the Bridge will be looking for us... if we even knew where the Bridge station *is* in this world."

"Both sides..." Matt began to think. "Yes... but the other side will be a lot better guarded, probably the Clinton Bridgeport. They'd be a lot happier grabbing us on our way out. No need to 'disappear' us here, less trouble with the local law... this side of the Bridge is probably pretty lightly watched..."

"Not seeing the point."

Matt laughed. "I'll look for an open position in the nerd patrol for you. What we need is to end up at an unguarded portal on the other side. Change the coordinates!"

Bobbi snorted. "Sure. No problem. I'll just get started building a Bridge right here, shall I? Ben, where do you keep the stone knives? Oh, and I'll need some bear skins."

Ben laughed. "Frank used to say things like that about ECHO. Is that some sort of common slang where you come from?"

"For sufficiently geeky values of 'common.'" Matt continued. "We don't need our own Bridge… just the right coordinates. Do you know the Vensky Equations?"

"Duh. Doesn't everyone? But good luck solving them for a given case *here*."

"What? You don't have a scientific calculator on your phone?"

She looked sheepish. "There's only, uh, so much room in active memory. I never really needed one, so I swapped it out for… uh… Tetris." She tried to meet his eyes. "Look, I get bored easily! Next time I configure it, I'll think to myself 'Gee, what if I get stuck in some backwater world and need to jury-rig a way off of it?' I promise!"

Matt looked at the papers scattered around them. "There is another option…"

She stared at him, slack jawed.

"You… are going to expect me… to rig up a wiring panel, no storage, vacuum tube driven monstrosity to handle the Vensky Bridge equations? While we're hunted fugitives? With only a vague idea of where we're going?"

Matt nodded.

"Cool! When do we start?"

The answer, as it turned out, was "tomorrow evening," which meant that Matt was able to enjoy a hot (well, lukewarm) shower and a full night's sleep for the first time in days, and then got to endure roughly twelve hours of dissertation on everything wrong with the universe in which they found themselves, from the labels on the cans of hash in the kitchen to the quality of the programs on the radio. A need to say something other than "You're right" or "Uh-huh" forced Matt to occasionally make a feeble semi-defense of this world's culture and values, such as they were, which invariably brought forth another round of vituperation (and the occasional reminder that this was all his fault).

Eventually, Matt stopped even trying to be patient. "Oh, for God's sake! Complaining and whining isn't going to get us out of here any faster! Welcome to the thrill a minute life of an FBI agent. You get five minutes of being shot at for every five weeks of sitting around bored out of your skill. I learned to deal, so can you!!"

"First, I'm *not* an FBI agent. Second… I'm just so… so… alone!"

"Gee, thanks."

"I mean… I'm totally cut off. From everything. I've never felt so… isolated. I mean, I think, 'Hey, I wonder if the President on this world was anyone half-important on ours, and I go to plug his name in a search engine, and I can't. Then I think, 'I wonder what the route to the army base is,' and I can't log on to a mapper to find that out. Then I figure I'll catch up on whatever shows I've missed and… you get the idea. I feel like I'm in a box."

Matt snorted. "So you've never had to endure a blackout or anything else which tore you away from your digital umbilical?"

"Once or twice, maybe. But then, you know, I could at least go find some friends, or even fire up a laptop or something. I can't even leave this dingy apartment, not that there's anything to see out there. And there's nothing to do in here, except read one of the maybe six books Ben had smuggled in from Prime, all of which I read to death before I was ten. Or I could look at more of those wiring diagrams."

"That actually seems like it might be vaguely productive. We aren't going to have a lot of time to run the equations, and the more you know about ECHO, the better. I'm not going to be a lot of use tonight."

Bobbi's glare contained the obvious reply to the straight line, but she gathered up some of the sheets of paper and sat down with a huff, then began to look over them. This didn't actually reduce the amount of complaining mixed with profanity, but it did give it a focus.

"Incredible… two thousand goddamn eight here and they've barely managed to perfect the vacuum tube… not even thinking about storage… aw, hell, can we even fit the algorithm to solve them into this thing… huh… this is going to take some thinking…"

Matt, meanwhile, amused himself with occasional glances out the window and brief flashes of panic whenever a police car drove by. Apparently, their escape had resulted in a temporary dead end, but he knew that sooner or later, they'd be tracked down. It wouldn't take them long to work out he was meeting someone on the fifth floor, and then get addresses and start looking for them. There was little doubt they'd find the information. Usually, low-tech worlds like this were lax about identification and the like, but this one, in the grip of a constant low-level xenophobia, probably had all sorts of laws about verifiable ID. While it was a lot harder to follow a paper trail without any kind of computers or telecommunication, it wasn't impossible, especially when the trail only led a few miles away.

Night fell with depressing slowness. Ben had returned with a bounty of food, if a bounty could be defined as small, flavorless, hamburgers and lumpy mashed potatoes. He explained his plan.

"It's not all that odd if one or two of us is working late on the project. The MPs don't really raise an eyebrow if the lights are on late, so all we've got to do is sneak you in."

Bobbi paused in her devouring. "Let me guess… more sewers."

"Huh? No, none of that. I've got a pickup trunk from my uncle. We can hide you in the back of it. I'll just tell the guard my other car has got a flat or something."

Bobbi got up and tromped into the kitchen, where she opened the refrigerator to see if, maybe, a bottle of ketchup had magically appeared in the five minutes since the last time she looked. It hadn't. Then she returned, sat down on the overstuffed sofa, and said, "I am not crawling through any air ducts."

Ben looked puzzled. Matt tried to stifle a laugh.

"Umm, air ducts? No, we just drive the pickup to building twelve, then…"

Matt waved for him to be silent. "No, no. What she means is, well, where we come from, the whole 'sneak in hiding in the back of a truck' thing is sort of, well, a cliché. So is crawling through air ducts to escape."

Ben pondered this a second. "Wouldn't any place you'd need to escape from be sure to make their ducts too small to crawl through?"

Bobbi laughed suddenly. "You may have a great career ahead of you as an evil overlord. Ghu knows, this world could use some excitement."

Ben figured it wasn't worth asking about.

The army base was fairly typical: a collection of low, squat, drab buildings, whose every lack of detail and design was highlighted by brilliant floodlights shining in all directions. Despite the tall guard towers and miles of barbed wire, though, the attitude expressed by the MP at the gate was one of bored complacency. He waved Ben through without even asking him where he'd got the truck. On a world defined by incuriosity and paranoia, Matt thought, you never know which trait is going to win out.

They parked in the dark shadow of building twelve, a place where the bright lights rarely reached. Ben waited until the darkness was at its peak, and then signaled for Matt and Bobbi to leave the truck. They made their way to the door.

Ben stopped for a second and listened. "What's that you're humming?"

Bobbi whispered back, "Just something from my world. Appropriate for this sort of sneaking around."

Matt snickered. "You really can't pass for Peter Graves."

"Peter who? Did you even *see* the movie?"

Matt sighed.

The door was opened. The room smelled of oil and machinery and burnt out tubes. Ben shut the door carefully then flipped on the lights. Bright illumination flooded down, revealing rows of machinery. Tall, cabinet like boxes stood in several parallel lines, hooked together by thick cables. Benches were covered with glass tubes, soldering irons, lengths of copper wire, and thick binders full of notes and diagrams.

Bobbi whistled. The setup was a lot less complete looking than she'd hoped.

"So, uh, how functional is this monster?"

Ben tapped one of the cases proudly. "Almost totally. We can run just about any calculation we want, once we've wired her up. There's just one small glitch..."

"There always is. What doesn't it do?"

"We're in the process of replacing the card typer. About a week ago, we realized there was a much better way to handle the output, so we gutted the old system and..."

"So we can run a program, but we can't see the results? Oh, great. As brilliant plans go..."

Ben stopped her. "No, no, we've got ways to see it... see those lights? They show the final state of the accumulators. So all you have to do is read them, and you've got your answers..."

Bobbi tried to decide if cursing or crying was more in order, then just shrugged and walked over to the first of the large wiring panels. "Okay, Ben, I know the math, and you know how to make this nightmare go. Let's get to work. Matt... just watch the blinking lights, okay?"

Matt sat down in a hard wooden chair and watched. When they make a movie of this, he thought, it's going to have a cool montage sequence for this part, with lots of fades and cuts and lasting about 15 seconds, because there's very little more boring than watching people plug wires into sockets.

"So, where do we want to end up?"

Matt woke from a half-sleep. "Umm... what?"

"I've got everything set up to solve the equations... except the solution we're solving for. Where are we planning on going?"

"Well, we'll need a receiver... there's no way to open an unsupported Bridge to Prime..."

Bobbi rolled her eyes. "And two and two is four. Please don't tell me any more stuff I learned in grade school, okay? What receiver? Do you have a top secret FBI platform somewhere?"

"Probably. The problem with being top secret is that folks in copyright enforcement generally aren't privy to it."

"So, what then?"

"Yours, of course! The BATS Bridge! You have to keep it open on standby mode, don't you, since you never know when someone will be coming through."

"Cops, remember? A raid? Which we jumped out ahead of?"

"Ess-Oh-Pee in such cases is to leave the Bridge functioning until everything can be traced and catalogued. It's probably still open."

"And if it's not?"

"Then we end up with our molecules scattered across a few dozen worlds. Do you have a better plan? Can't you, of all people, trust that the police will dutifully follow procedure to the tedious letter?"

"Alright, but only because I'd rather be scattered across time and space then be stuck in this hellhole one more day." She turned to begin wiring in the final parameters.

"Wait!" Matt stood up suddenly. "Let me see your phone!"

Confused, she handed it to him. Matt flipped it open and began pushing buttons, his expression growing more and more baffled with each second. "Categories... programs ... data... menu... utilities... catalog... augh!" He handed it back to her. "Show me what you pulled from Frank's computer. The coordinates."

She tapped the phone twice. "There. Not very hard."

He glanced at the rows of numbers and notes, wondering briefly what "Hot Slut High" might refer to, then deciding he didn't want to know. He scrolled down to Oz.

```
Oz, Prison (UnSup) 46.2 α, 71.1 β, 90.09 γ, 205.12 δ
Oz, WWOW   (UnSup) 46.4 α, 71.2 β, 85.09 γ, 204.11 δ
Oz, EmCit   (Sup)  46.3 α, 71.1 β, 85.12 γ, 200.15 δ
```

"Bobbi, can you get this thing to perform an inversion, given one set of supported coordinates?"

"Umm, sure, but it will take a while. Why?"

"We're heading for the other side of the rainbow... the Prime side of the Emerald City Bridge."

"So we can get arrested at home? Great plan."

"They won't chance it. They're expecting us to run for either the Topeka or Oz portals. The other side of the Topeka is where they hope to grab us – there'll be no one there, pretty much, to see it. The Oz portal on Prime is a major tourist stop, so they've got huge crowds there, but they've got enough pull in Emerald City to get us yanked long before we get there. So we lay our own Bridge, from Topeka here to the Oz gateway there, and with a little luck, we're home with a little time to plot our next move."

"So what *is* our next move?"

He told her.

She nodded. "Cute. Probably work, too. You know, for a government tool, you've got a certain odd sense of style." She then turned back to complex maze of wires that she and Ben had been laboriously assembling. "Gotta rip out about half of this now. Shit."

Another hour passed, during which two tubes needed to replaced and a few loose connections hastily soldered together. "Sorry, we weren't totally done with the square root unit... a few last minute changes..."

Matt set aside the soldering iron. "It's alright, Ben. Is that the last bit? Are we good to go?"

Ben looked back at the machine. "Yes, I think we are. Umm..."

"What?"

"Isn't this... uh... some sort of secret. With these formulas... couldn't we build a, what do you call them, a Bridge of our own? I mean, even if we don't have the technology yet, the math is the hard part..."

Bobbi laughed. Matt explained. "This just calculates a landing point. It's not anywhere near the full equation. And even if you could derive the rest of the math... it wouldn't do you any good."

Ben seemed miffed. "Why not? I know you think we're stupid here, but we're not. Just a little... behind you."

"It's not that. It's the Vensky Inconstant."

"Inconstant?"

"A little joke. There's a key value to the equations which is... wrong... everywhere but Prime. We can build Bridges out, and open Bridges back... but no one else can, at least, no one we've ever found, and the best solution anyone's found to the Second Vensky Theorem says that no other universe can have the same value for the Inconstant. So all roads lead to... and from... Prime."

"Oh."

Bobbi chirped in. "Hey, enough exposition. Let's get this thing running!"

Ben walked over to a tall cabinet. "Okay, got it. Initializing run. Go."

There was disappointing lack of effect. No sparks climbed up and down antennae, there was no sudden dimming of the lights, and there was a total absence of an ominous rising hum. There was nothing but a slight ozone smell and the faint hiss and crack of primitive electronics, which went on and on for quite a while.

"Is it working?"

Bobbi nodded. "Looks like it is. See, the accumulators are going full tilt." She gestured to one set of blinking lights. "And you can see core memory filling up." A finger pointed to another set of what Matt thought were identical lights. "We didn't have time to add a little progress bar reading 'Important Equations Calculation Now 56% done.'"

"Progress bar?"

"Never mind, Ben. Wait a second," Matt said. "God, I'm an idiot."

Bobbi looked away from the display of light for a moment. "I agree, but what did you do now?"

"We need to know where this Bridge is located!"

Bobbi slammed her head into a panel, which fortunately did not disconnect any wires. "Well, that was brilliant of us."

Matt turned back to Ben. "Ben, do you have any idea where the Bridge is? Where Frank came from?"

Ben nodded. "I… think I might know. We'd always met Frank by the Brown Street Hotel. I thought it was because it was cheap, but maybe…" He shrugged.

"It's our best chance. You have a map here? Can you show me how to get there?"

"Sure." The streets were laid out very simply, and Matt could easily see the route he'd need to take. He committed it to memory, despite Ben's insistence he'd be happy to drive them there.

Matt wandered to the window. The hour was late, without even a trace of dawn on the horizon. Nothing but the slow pan of the searchlights and the flickering red and blue of…

"Ben! Do you normally get the local cops up here?"

"No, of course not. The MPs deal with most trouble. They'd only be here if there was some kind of civilian involvement."

"You mean, like wanted fugitives hanging out near top-secret equipment?"

Ben nodded. "Yes, that would do it."

"Bobbi! Are those damn equations done yet?"

"Almost… just gotta input the numbers!" She was staring at the readout board, frantically converting binary values and tapping them into her phone. "Okay… last one… got it! Let's go!"

Matt turned to Ben. "You got your truck keys?"

He held them out. "Right here. We can—"

"Thanks. It's a real shame how we had to hold you at gunpoint and forced you to let us do all this."

Ben was caught in mid-sentence. "Huh? You didn't—"

He was cut off as Matt punched him in the jaw and then followed up with a stunning blow to the neck. He collapsed, coughing blood.

Bobbi looked shocked. "Hey, even *I* didn't want to hit him. He's about the only sane person we've met in this cesspit of a world."

"Right, and do you want him tossed in a military jail or just shot as a spy? Or maybe you figured you'd smuggle him home with us?"

"So, fine. You've knocked out our only ally here. Now what?"

"We add grand theft auto to our list of crimes."

"The fourth one sucked."

"Huh? Never mind. Come on, the truck's this way."

They raced for the truck and hopped in. Matt turned the key

and then struggled to remember how to drive a manual transmission, even as the police cars were drawing closer.

"It doesn't help that all the controls are in just the wrong place!" He raised his hands in frustration.

Bobbi peered over at the driver's side. "Seen a lot of different car layouts in my time. Cross-world car rental... don't even ask me about the insurance rate. Anyway, look, there's the clutch, pull it... okay, ease onto the gas... whoa!" She fell back to her side rather ungracefully.

Matt stated the obvious. "Hey, we're moving!"

"I'm pretty surprised myself. Where to?"

"The local Bridge, of course. Brown Street Hotel. We make a left out there, then straight for about two miles..." He began to move the car towards the base's entrance.

Bobbi looked ahead, seeing what was shown in the headlight's glow. "You, uh, notice there's a gate in the way?"

Matt grinned wickedly. "Not for long!"

Matt kicked the pickup ahead two gears. It protested mightily, lurched, and accelerated. He smashed down on the horn continuously, trying to get the guards at the gate to duck out of the way. Most did, but drew rifles in the process and began to open fire. Bullets tore through the truck, mostly impacting harmlessly.

Mostly.

Just as the truck breached the gate, carrying it forward about twenty feet before it finally fell free, one bullet smashed through the rear of the cab and into Bobbi.

"Shit!" she screamed and put her hand to her shoulder. It came away scarlet.

"Damn... God... ow, that hurts like a mother... oh God, am I going to die? I'm going to die, aren't I?"

Matt spared a second from navigating the maze of darkened streets to glance over at her. "Not if we get you to any kind of decent hospital. Looks like a shoulder wound. Don't think it hit anything vital, but you're bleeding pretty badly. Try to staunch it with something."

"With what?"

"I don't know! Little busy trying to lose the cops here!"

Bobbi tried to turn to look behind them, lifting herself with her wounded arm as she did so. Then she screamed again.

"Don't put any weight on that arm."

"Now you... tell... me."

Matt looked around frantically. "There! Just behind you, on that hook. Some coveralls or something. Wrap the wound in them, anything to try to slow down the blood loss."

She grabbed them with her other arm. "Ugh! These are filthy!"

"We've got antibiotics on Prime! We've just got to get there!"

Clumsily, and with much profanity, she began to tie off the wound. The truck slowed down. "Okay, get out here."

"What? Why?"

"Just do it! Now!"

Bobbi, too weak from pain and blood loss to argue much, staggered out of the truck.

"Okay, here goes nothing!" Matt pressed down hard on the gas, then, as the vehicle accelerated, flung open the door and leapt out. Seconds later, the truck careened off a bridge and into the river below.

He stood up, wincing somewhat from the pain in his left side. *That looks so much easier on TV*, he thought, and rejoined Bobbi. "There. That will hopefully keep the cops a little busy. Two blocks that way."

Bobbi had spent most of her off-world time on the Bridges to the mainline worlds – the tourist worlds where England still ruled America and everything was quaintly British, the industrial exploitation worlds where the biosphere was so damaged that not even the most fanatical Luddite could whine about strip mining, the residence worlds where humanity never developed, the altstyle worlds where the 60s free love movement was never battered by cynicism or disease, and, of course, the low-deltas, the near-parallels where she did most of her work. She wondered, sometimes, what the Bridges to the backwaters were like, the way someone might look at a map and see a tiny symbol for a town on a tiny island somewhere in the North Sea and wonder what it might be like to live there. Now she knew. The answer was "Terrifyingly dull."

Mainline Bridges are bustling places. Security guards monitor the Bridge itself. Signs and shops advertise every kind of amenity a traveler might need. There are currency exchanges if the world has currency, and ways to get the appropriate brightly colored shells or healthy chickens if the barter system is in effect. Medical clinics if the traveler needs shots, or if he needs to be checked for something... like the way Carter-2 is lethal to anyone with a peanut allergy. Luggage searches. Native guides looking for employment, if the natives are allowed to know about the Bridges.

The Topeka Bridge in the world Bobbi had mentally labeled Kansas-666 was located in the back room of a seedy downtown hotel, the idea being, it seemed, that it would not be odd to see strangers entering and leaving such a place. A hand painted "No Vacancy" sign hung over the front door, and a tired clerk reclined behind the front desk. Bobbi thought that by the way his shoulders were moving, he had some sort of handheld video game hidden below the counter. At least, she hoped he did.

When he saw them, though, he began to react, reaching for something. He stopped when Matt moved away from supporting the injured Bobbi and showed off the crimson and gold pistol, then pressed a finger to his lips. Bobbi and Matt moved towards the unmarked wooden door behind the clerk. Matt turned the handle, tested the door very gently to make sure it wasn't bolted or locked from the other side, then kicked it open and yelled "Freeze! Nobody move, and nobody gets hurt!"

Bobbi rolled her eyes. "Have you been waiting your whole life to say that?"

Matt kept his eyes, and his gun, pointed at the two men near the Bridge console. "You're ruining my moment here, you know that?"

"Whatever. I'm bleeding to death. Can the dramatics." She then turned to the two men. "Right, you heard your co-worker. Move away from the controls. I'm shot, I'm hungry, I'm tired, my feet are fucking killing me, I haven't had any coffee *or* chocolate in three days and I don't like any of you people anyway. So move!"

They moved.

Bobbi glanced around the room itself. A Bridge terminal, a 4-man size, occupied the far wall. A desk which handled all the bureaucratic functions needed for this entire world sat near the door. A pamphlet rack, dust covered, advertised the many attractions of this world. It was about ten percent full. A faded and curling poster noted the standard Bridge regulations. The Bridge control panel was in the center of the room. Bobbi walked to it.

They hadn't even bothered a standard lockdown.

She flipped open her phone clumsily, trying to work it one-handed. There were the correct coordinates. She typed them in, trying to ignore the alternating numbness and pain in her injured arm. The system accepted the numbers, and there was a faint whirr as the parantennae in the Bridge aligned to the new settings.

She set the timer on the Bridge, then stopped and smiled. If they'd left the security set to defaults, like lazy, bored, complacent people usually do… they had. Even as Matt gestured frantically for her to speed up, she entered a command sequence. "Okay, let's go! Ten second timer from *now*!" she said, even as the boringly familiar wail of police sirens was becoming audible outside.

Matt raced towards the Bridge, as the two guards grabbed for their own guns and the door broke down, He barely saw the local cops trying to aim and fire when the world changed.

They were on a large platform, five or six time bigger than the one they'd just departed. Uniformed men and women watched them appear, and began to gesture for them to clear the plate, when they saw the way Bobbi was slumped against Matt, the bloodstains on her shirt clearly visible. There was a murmur and a growing unease. Oz was not supposed to be dangerous.

"Make way, step aside, we've got an injury here!" He began to slowly leave the platform, Bobbi behind him. He whispered back to her. "Are you doing it?"

"Yeah. Got the lock on… beginning… we'll need a few minutes. Five, tops."

"Right."

He turned to the crowd. About half were dressed in typical Prime garb, which meant everything from business suits to thought-sensing body paint. The others were done up in the latest Oz fashions. All were clearly frightened and confused. Good, he thought. I need to get out of here. He led Bobbi to the nearest guard. "Here, she needs help. What are you waiting for? Isn't there a trauma team here?"

"Uh, no, we've got an RN and we've all had first aid training but…"

"Well, do something! She's bleeding!"

The guard flipped open his phone and began to make the necessary calls. Matt merged into the milling throng. Dimly, he heard the guard behind him calling out "Wait, sir… we need to ask you…"

Matt ignored him and pushed through the crowd, rushing past the stores, booths, and so on. One place was rather enterprisingly selling "Witch Repellent," thirty cent plastic water pistols marked up to twenty dollars. People bought them because they were "cute." Another store specialized in color-coordinated outfits for each of the four regions. A spinner rack held small books promising "One Hundred Useful Phrases and Idioms." Extremely cheap and flimsy umbrellas were being sold at ludicrous prices beneath an image of a flying monkey defecating from the sky. Mostly people just ambled by the displays, but there was a wave of panic and confusion, a rock of chaos tossed into the pond of apathy, and people began to move and jog for position, some straining to see what was going on at the Bridge, others pulling back and away lest it be something dangerous. Fear and curiosity, twin monkey (flying or otherwise) instincts at war. Matt just shoved through, ignoring curses and imprecations hurled at him.

Okay. It won't be long before this gets to the authorities and they get here. So it's time to go somewhere they probably aren't thinking I'll go...

There was police tape on the door, but it was torn. Matt tested the handle. Open.

The large warehouse used by the BATS had always been a maze of technology and strange devices; now the maze was draped in yellow tape. A handful of tags and labels had been scattered onto the machines like falling leaves; a few were plastered with stickers for biohazard, radiation, and one with a clock striking thirteen, the new symbol for 'Chronological Instability Risk'. Matt's eyes widened at that; he didn't think the BATS were bringing over stuff that risky, even if it allegedly was non-functional under Prime laws. At least he didn't see any "Pi=4" stickers; those scared him.

His entry hadn't been quiet; there were noises in return. A voice called out.

"Jason?"

Matt contemplated not answering, in order to try to get him to say more, but responded anyway. "No. It's Matt."

There was a sudden clatter of things dropping. Matt moved towards it, gun drawn.

Julius was standing, looking more out of sorts than Matt had ever seen him, by the Bridge controls. The controlling computer was showing a static image; Matt guessed it was a password dialog.

He regained composure quickly. It was his primary skill; the ability to always seem to be on top of things. The appearance of competence was always more important than the real thing.

"Oh. Good to see you. Was doing a little work down here, seeing what's in our jurisdiction. Um... you know you're wanted, right? I saw the reports... very confusing. You attacked Brian?" He forced a smile which he clearly intended to be friendly. "Well, I've known you for years. I'm sure whatever's happening, we can work it all out."

Matt sighed and sneered at the same time. "Oh, drop the innocent act, Julius. You're really not fooling anyone."

"About what?"

"About anything. You know. You – or someone else in copyright, doesn't really matter – saw Frank visiting that backwater and wanted to check it out to see what he was after. I don't know how you found the Oz connection, but you did, and you realized you had a smuggling route no one would suspect. So you cut some deal with the borg chimp, he set up the workshops, you collected the output, and flew it over to Kansas and sent it from there to wherever magic heroin would sell. Pretty nice, until one of them got away and made it back here. Then, you tried to cover your tracks, and failed, it's all been in free fall since then."

Julius tried to game on. "An... ah... interesting story. An amusing attempt to cover up the near murder of a fellow agent. I didn't really think this sort of thing was in your psych profile, though. I, um, I will put in a good word about your years of dedicated..."

Matt had drawn the pistol he'd been carrying since Oz.

"I know it's a rather colorful little gun, but it's still a gun, and pretty bullets kill you just as dead."

Julius backed away slightly, stumbling against the computer desk. "You're not helping your case any. Look. I can help you. I can. Just tell me... have you explained this fairy tale to anyone else yet?"

Matt paused a moment. "No, not personally. I haven't."

Julius looked relieved. He smiled and took a step forward. Then something seemed to tick in his mind.

"What do you mean 'not personally'?"

Matt smiled. "You might want to check out BobbisBlog. One word. That's bee-eye-ess-bee. Right."

Julius turned to the desk, ignoring the main PC, and activated a smaller computer. Matt recognized it as Julius' Bureau-issued laptop. *Bet* that's *got a lot of good stuff on it,* Matt thought.

The small screen filled with an assortment of captioned photos and brief film clips, in surprisingly high resolution. The munchkin town, Sergeant Whisk... then the shots of the prison, the workrooms, the mangled corpse left behind in the woods, a few pictures of Kansas, and on and on. Quite a few, Matt realized, of himself, always looking flustered, confused, startled, or slack-jawed. *Well, I suppose my dreams of coming out of this looking like a square jawed action hero were pretty misplaced. Hm. I never realized my left ear stuck out like that.* He rubbed it, suddenly self-conscious.

Julius watched the cavalcade of images, his frown deepening and a slight sheen of sweat beginning to form. *We can still manage this. We can take this down quickly*, he thought. *At least it's one obscure little page out of billions. Not really a problem...*

Matt could see which way his mind was running. He decided to cut off that particular line of reasoning. "Oh, and Videorama, of course. Infinipedia... I think it's on the Oz page, though it might be linked to the FBI by now... also FBIWatch, I know, I hate those commies too, but needs must and all that. Also..."

Julius slammed the laptop shut and turned to Matt, face genuinely angry – among the first real emotion Matt had ever seen him express.

"We can tear this down. Everything... easily faked. A week with some image editing software and special effects..."

Matt couldn't help grinning. "Did I mention Bobbi owns a courtroom-certified camera? And even if you stole the camera, the hardware key is on file with the company. They're all real and we can prove it."

Julius's mind seemed to spin out into a void. He was one of those people who rehearsed every possible thread of a conversation and had a ready response to it, but he was quite suddenly caught off guard, his mental algorithm collapsing into a maze of null pointers. He shoved a tray of wrenches, gears, and spools of wire towards Matt, then spun and bolted deeper into the warehouse.

Matt wasn't sure what to expect, but thirty-odd pounds of assorted metal flying at his face wasn't it. He threw his arm up, but a Heterodyne Type-3 Wide Spanner still managed to clonk him on the forehead. There was a moment of dizziness, followed by the feeling of a thin, warm, trickle down his face. He looked around.

Julius was not visible, but Matt didn't think he'd left the building. Right now, the Bridge here was his only hope.

He looked. The place was a dimly lit maze, and the chaos of the firefight during their initial escape hadn't helped matters much. He stood still, and listened. There was a slight sound to the left, a faint scuffling. He moved that way, as quietly as he could.

Julius was standing still, almost. He was at the base of something which looked like it was made from brass, crystal, and seashells. It had a long projecting nozzle and was mounted on a series of... somethings... that looked partially like gears and partially like twisting ribbons of metal. There was a soft, musical, hum as it began to glow. He spun it towards Matt. There was a brilliant flare of light, and a bright beam of red energy emerged from it, slicing through the air and hitting Matt directly in the chest. Matt staggered back and looked down, expecting to see a gaping, charred, hole, but the beam simply stopped. He felt, at most, slightly warm. He looked up at Julius. Both looked sheepish. Matt, ignoring the non-deadly beam, cocked his head slightly.

"Isn't that... isn't that the Martian weapon from Kipling's 'Ballad of Syria Planum'?"

Julius glanced down at a tag. "Kipling from V-12, yes. Damn it, it's marked functional." He looked somewhat petulantly at Matt. "You should be very dead."

Matt shrugged. "Around here, 'functional' means 'will not explode when you touch it'."

"Idiots. I can't believe we're arresting them for arms smuggling. It's like locking people up for smuggling water pistols."

Matt edged closer. "Well, you remember that Smith & Wesson hydro-accelerator someone brought back. Could cut a man in half at fifty yards."

Julius nodded, and then shoved the surprisingly useless Martian laser towards Matt, who parried it. It went flying, collapsing and crashing in an oddly musical tinkle of broken glass. Matt sighed.

"Julius, just give it up! This is going to get silly. Sillier. God damn it, I've been dealing with talking buckets and my feet hurt and I'm starving. Why are you dragging this out?"

Julius paused, seeking reason. Matt could watch his brain working, calculating, weighing all the angles and options. He'd seen that mind working many times, watched him puzzle down a dozen paths and consider all the branches, recursively pruning one decision tree after another. There was only one option left that was safe and sane, and that would be to surrender, confess, and plea bargain, trading all the dirty secrets he'd learned in years of work for a reduction here, a lenience there, ending with a few years in a Club Fed on some comfortable remote Offworld and a tell-all memoir a decade down the road.

That was the only intelligent option.

Julius hurled a massive set of golden gears at Matt. Matt twisted partly out of the way but was still grazed by it. It impacted heavily on his skull and his vision exploded to bright flashes. Julius seized the moment and raced back for the Bridge.

Matt followed him a moment later. *At least this time, I'm doing the chasing,* he thought. From somewhere ahead, he heard a loud whine and a strange squeal. He followed it, passed a pile of charred and molten metal and a small, handwritten tag on the floor. He stopped to look at it, shook his head, and laughed silently.

Julius was still at the console, which had finally unlocked. He spun when he heard Matt approach, the Bridge powering up behind him. A gun was in his hand, all translucent crystal and shimmering chrome.

"Chinese icebreaker program. Great stuff." He kicked a rolling tool case towards Matt, who dodged around and it and pressed forward.

"Why bother? We can track you. You know all this. It's your job." Matt stepped towards Julius, who raised the gun.

"This one *really* works. I tested it. I've set the console to wipe as soon as the Bridge closed. Hell, even I don't know where I'm going. Random settings. I don't want to shoot you, Matt, but I will. I can't go back, can't face it all. A few more weeks... I would have had enough. Managed to get out. Now... time to start over."

Matt sighed and raised his own gun. "You're just making it worse for yourself."

"I'm sorry, Matt." Julius fired. Or, at least, tried to. There was a clicking noise and nothing happened. He tried again, and this time, the gun began to glow brightly. Julius screamed in pain and dropped it, his hand already red and blistering. He spun and tried to leap for the Bridge.

Matt fired.

And hit the parantennae. The dimensional lock was lost. The

Bridge's safety systems – Matt was slightly surprised it had any – tripped, triggering an instant shutdown. Julius landed on the pad, trapped. He glowered at the discarded gun, which was now a dull grey, the crystal cracked and useless.

Matt glanced at it briefly. "Isher weapon. Only useful in self-defense. Won't fire on a law officer performing what it considers to be a legitimate arrest. "

Julius slumped, defeated. "I hate nerds."

A week later, Matt looked around happily. He had an office, not a cubicle, and it was in Fugitive Tracking. Partly it was a reward to please the media, and partly it was because they figured anyone with experience dodging the cops across three worlds would be good at the job.

He was in the process of getting his email set up (and wondering why he couldn't have just kept his old system) when Bobbi walked in. The only evidence of her injury was a small pad which made a tiny bulge under her T-shirt (black, of course, with a joke on it Matt didn't get and didn't want to).

"You... uh... seem to be healing well. Uh... how is the lawsuit going?"

She smiled. "I can't talk to you about it, duh. You work for the people I'm suing. Well, some of the people I'm suing. I'll be lucky to get half my shit back intact when this mess is all over. I'm crashing with Karen for now, and it's one hell of a mess. Never live with your friends."

"Oh. okay. Umm, I did try to call a few times..."

"Yeah, I know. Look. Despite what you think, the fact we spent a couple of days romping across assorted worlds, defying death, solving mysteries, and *getting shot*" – she spit out the last two words – "does not mean we're automatically romantically linked. One adventure doesn't buy you a relationship."

"I didn't think..."

"But it does entitle you to buy me dinner. You're earning Commandant money now; you can take me someplace decent. Karen's only cooking utensil is a microwave." She didn't wait for him to answer, but looked around.

"So, new digs, I take it? This is what you wanted, right?

Fugitive tracking?"

"Yes. No more nerd patrol. Now it's all *sane* stuff. Murderers fleeing justice. Robbers trying to launder their loot across dimensions. Doppelganger-killers. No flying monkeys, illegal science fiction clubs, or talking buckets for me anymore. Sanity. Good, clear, criminal, sanity."

Bobbi shrugged. "Right, whatever. I'm hungry. Are we going?" She flashed a smile that contained some actual warmth.

Matt nodded. "Let me get my coat. Good thing about being a Commandant, I can take lunch when I want."

The door opened. It was Johnson? Jackson? Something like that. His new underling. Matt enjoyed the thought of underlings.

"I was heading out, uh..."

"Jameson, sir."

"Right, I was heading out for lunch, Mr. Jameson, so..."

"This really can't wait, sir. It's a pretty urgent dispatch."

"Oh for the love of... well, what is it?"

"Someone's killed Superman."

About the Author

Ian ("Lizard") Harac is a longtime science fiction fan and Alpha Nerd. After 20 or so years of waiting for someone to spontaneously offer him writing gigs, he actually started submitting things, and discovered, to his surprise, that people liked them and bought them.

He began his writing career in 2000 and became a well-known freelancer in the gaming business, working on many products for *Dungeons & Dragons*, *GURPS*, and the *Dying Earth*. This is first published fiction, and he hopes not his last. He currently lives in Indiana, where he shares a small house with one beloved wife and five usually-beloved cats.

Also from Ian Harac...

MEDIC!

by Ian Harac

After the apocalypse, nothing is left but mad robots, madder life forms, and desperate survivors. Doctor MacIntyre, a self-aware ambulance, acts as a freelance medic offering help to those who need it. In this violent, desperate world, MacIntyre can rely on nothing but his wits, his uneasy allies... and a few missile racks he had installed, just in case. He battles violent fanatics, would-be conquerors, and a force that would snuff out any hope of a future.
[Snarky Apocalyptic Sci-Fi 14+]

THE WRECK OF ALPHA CENTRAL

roleplaying in an alien post-apocalyptic future

Ecumenopolis, the world city. Science fiction is full of them, from Trantor to Coruscant.But then it all stops working.

What happens to a world of 40 trillion people when the food shipments stop and the lights go out?

Post-apocalyptic mutants, aliens, freaks, weirdos, dangers, and wonders abound.
[HERO System Roleplaying]

www.blackwyrm.com

Also from BlackWyrm...

TRAJAN'S ARCH

Gabriel Rackett has written one novel and has no prospects of writing another, his powers stagnated by drink and loss. Into his possession comes a childhood friend's manuscript, taking him back to the ghosts that haunted his own coming-of-age. Gabriel returns to his old haunts through a series of fantastic stories that preoccupy and pursue him back to their dark secret sources.
[Fantasy Realism, ages 18+]

PAST LIVES

by Christopher Kokoski

Secrets, Mystery, Destiny
Plunged into the center of a high-profile murder investigation, Eric Shooter discovers under hypnosis that he is a reincarnated serial killer. The only way to clear his name is to track down the most elusive and cunning predator in history, a methodical assassin with whom he shares a shocking connection.
[Paranormal Mystery, ages 14+]

www.blackwyrm.com

The Starcrossed

by William I. Levy

What are the odds of meeting your soulmate sixty light years away from home on the very first expedition to another star system?

Not as good as the chance of getting killed by a military conspiracy, renegade scientists, or a demonic entity from beyond time. But Barret and Paum have found something special. And they're not going to let a little thing like Armageddon stand in the way. Hopefully.

[Sci-Fi Action Romance, ages 18+]

by Brad Parnell

Young Robert journeys to another world. There he comes of age amid a feuding government, grotesque monsters, an ancient ancestor ...and a couple of teenaged girls. With the help of a young wolf named Louie, Robert is introduced to the wonders and perils of a strange land called Gwerinatha.

[Allegoric Fantasy, ages 12+]

www.blackwyrm.com